ROCKY MOUNTAIN RESCUE

BROTHERHOOD PROTECTORS COLORADO BOOK #2

ELLE JAMES

TWISTED PAGE INC

ROCKY MOUNTAIN RESCUE

BROTHERHOOD PROTECTORS COLORADO
BOOK #2

New York Times & USA Today
Bestselling Author

ELLE JAMES

Dedicated to my mother and father who helped shape me into the person I am today.

Elle James

AUTHOR'S NOTE

Enjoy other military books by Elle James

Brotherhood Protectors Colorado
SEAL Salvation (#1)
Rocky Mountain Rescue (#2)
Ranger Redemption (#3)
Tactical Takeover (#4)
Shadow Assassin (crossover)

Visit ellejames.com for titles and release dates
For hot cowboys, visit her alter ego Myla Jackson at
mylajackson.com
and join Elle James's Newsletter at
https://ellejames.com/contact/

PROLOGUE

SOMETHING SCRATCHED AT HER LEG.

Then it happened again—pawing, digging, irritating.

She tried to kick her leg to make it stop. However, her legs wouldn't move, and the digging, scratching and pawing continued. When she attempted to move her arms, she couldn't. Her arms and legs would barely budge.

The little effort she expended drained her. Every breath she took weighed heavily on her lungs. Dust filled her nostrils. When she tried to open her eyes, everything was dark. She closed them again. It was too much effort to keep them open. Too much effort to breathe or move. Lying there, she wondered if it would be easier to stop breathing, stop moving and simply go to sleep. Forever.

The scratching stopped. The sound of something

sniffing near her ear was followed by more pawing. This time on the top of her head. Something caught in her hair and pulled.

She tried to turn her head away and tried to raise her arm and slap away whatever was pawing her. A whining sound accompanied the scratching. She didn't want to wake. She wanted to stay asleep, but the persistent pawing made her want to slap away whatever bothered her.

When she tried again to move her arm, this time it shifted just a little. Then it was free. She batted at the thing that punished her head with pawing.

Teeth wrapped around her hand and tugged.

A moan rose up her parched throat. She tried to tell the creature to leave her alone, but her mouth wouldn't open, her eyes wouldn't open. She willed it away, but it persisted.

Darkness faded into light. Warmth permeated her body, chasing away the chill. She moved her head to the side, and dirt shifted off her face exposing it to what felt like sunlight. When she opened her eyes this time the bright glare of sunrise hit her full on. She closed her eyes again.

Teeth sank into her fingers and pulled hard. The whining continued, and a sharp bark sounded in her ear. This time when she opened her eyes, she saw a long snout and a pair of dark eyes staring down at her. The teeth released her hand and the barking continued. The creature latched onto her wrist and pulled, forcing her to roll over. Once lying on her back, she was able to take a deep breath. Again, the animal released her hand and barked and barked and barked.

With each bark, pain radiated through her head. "Please stop. Please," she said. "*Stoooop.*"

It was a dog. The dog ignored her entreaty and continued to bark. Suddenly, it ran away, and silence reigned.

She lay with the sun beating down on her until she couldn't stand it anymore, and she raised her arm to cover her eyes. She must have fallen asleep again.

Voices woke her in a language she didn't understand. Her skin burned in the sunlight. Then a shadow fell over her, and she curled into the fetal position, expecting whoever it was to hit or kick her. Instead, someone draped fabric over her body.

More voices spoke in a language she did not understand. Too tired to open her eyes, she lay still, praying they'd go away. Someone lifted her head and poured water into her mouth. She gulped it thirstily. By the gentle strength in her hands and her soft voice, the person had to be a woman. The others had the same kinds of voices. They were all women. One tried to get her to sit up, but she lay back down, closing her eyes to the harshness of the sun. They left her alone.

After a while—how long, she didn't know—a

different voice sounded. Deeper, rougher. "Ma'am?" A hand touched her shoulder.

She whimpered and covered her face with her hand.

The dog was back. Its nose pressed against her cheek, and a long tongue licked the dirt from her face.

"Go on," the voice said.

The dog quit licking her.

"Ma'am, can you hear me? Do you speak English?" the voice asked.

Finally, a language she understood. "Yes," she said, her voice more of a crackling sound than anything else.

"We're going to move you. Ma'am, I'm a medic. Can you tell me your name?"

She blinked her eyes open and looked up into the face of a man.

When the man put his hands on her arms, she tried to fight him, but her arms and legs wouldn't move or work the way they used to.

"No," she said, "*Nooo*." She waved her arms at him, but they did no good. They were too weak to fight.

"It's okay, ma'am. I'm only going to move you," he said, his voice soothing.

"Please," she whispered. "Don't hurt me."

"I'm trying to help you." He looked over his shoulder. "Hey, Johnson, get over here."

"Please, don't hurt me," she murmured, every deep breath shooting pain through her chest.

The man above her turned to somebody else. "Talk to her, Johnson. Maybe it'll help if she has a female to speak to."

A woman wearing an Army desert sand uniform leaned over her and smoothed the hair back from her forehead. "Hey, I'm Specialist Johnson. We're here to help you. Can you tell me your name?"

She thought and she thought. Name. I have to have a name. I know my name, it's right on the tip of my tongue. What is my name?

"Ma'am, can you tell me your name?" Johnson said.

Tears welled in her eyes and slipped down her cheeks. "I don't…know."

The dog whined, snuck up close to her and pressed his snout to her face.

"Oh, sweetie," Johnson said. "Don't worry. You'll remember. The main thing is to get you somewhere safe so you can heal."

"Come on," the man said. "Let's get her on the stretcher and into the chopper."

Men lifted her and laid her on a stretcher. She fought until they strapped her down. The dog tried to jump on the stretcher with her.

"It must be hers. Take it with you," a man said.

The woman named Johnson scooped the dog up

into her arms and carried it with her as they loaded her onto the helicopter.

Then someone stuck a needle into her arm. Sunlight dimmed and darkness overtook her. As consciousness faded to black, her name came to her, and she whispered, "JoJo."

CHAPTER 1

"Could you hand me that crescent wrench so I can tighten this bolt?" Josephine Angelica Barrera-Ramirez, or JoJo, held out one hand while holding parts together with the other.

Gunny rattled around in the toolbox and then slapped a crescent wrench into her open palm. "I can't believe you got this old clunker running."

JoJo took the wrench and fitted it to the bolt. "A little elbow grease and some new parts are usually all it takes."

"When I was on active duty, they didn't have females in the motor pool." The retired Marine gunnery sergeant, Dan Tate, shook his head.

JoJo tightened the bolt, and then stood and straightened with a grin. "Well, maybe they should have. You would've been better off."

Gunny chuckled. "You could be right there. I don't think there's anything you can't fix."

JoJo hadn't met a machine she couldn't fiddle with and make run. Machines were easy.

People...were a different story.

She'd never really been good at relationships, even before she'd gone into the Army, and in the Army... Well, that's why she was going to a therapist. Thankfully, she was going to one Gunny had recommended. It helped to have another female she hadn't known before the Army to talk to. Sure, RJ, Gunny's daughter, would gladly let JoJo have a shoulder to lean or cry on, but some things were just too personal and too raw to share with her best friend. Although Emily, her therapist, was becoming more like a friend every day.

Still, they hadn't had a breakthrough in the past six months. Emily said that she might never overcome the amnesia brought on by the attack. She said that her mind was protecting her by keeping that door closed.

The problem was that JoJo couldn't get closure on the whole incident because she didn't know who had done it and why. And whoever had raped, beaten her and buried her out in the desert was still loose. As long as he was free, JoJo couldn't be free of the nightmares or being afraid of the dark. Until they put that man behind bars, she wouldn't be able to move on. In the meantime, she'd remain an emotional mess. Which bugged the crap out of her.

JoJo liked to think she was pretty tough, but that incident had destroyed her confidence in her ability to defend herself. Yes, Army basic training had taught her the basics of hand-to-hand combat, but a five-foot-nothing female who weighed maybe ninety-nine pounds soaking wet didn't stand a chance against a man who weighed over two hundred pounds. She still didn't like being alone with men.

With Gunny being the exception. As teenagers she and RJ had been the best of friends. She'd spent much of her time at RJ and Gunny's place when they'd lived in Colorado Springs. Gunny was like a second father to her. She and RJ had signed up for the Army on the same day, hoping for the buddy program. But that wasn't to be. RJ had been denied entry, based on medical reasons. JoJo had gone into the Army alone.

After tightening the bolt, JoJo straightened and climbed up into the seat of the old tractor. When she turned the key, the engine rumbled, coughed and finally sprang to life.

Gunny hooted and yelled, "Hallelujah!"

JoJo smiled. It always felt good to do something for Gunny. He'd done so much for her. He and RJ had taken her in when she'd gotten out of the Army. Gunny had given her a job and paid her a living wage, even when he really couldn't afford to. He'd even paid for her lessons in Krav Maga, an Israeli-style self-defense course, to help rebuild her confidence when she'd had none after leaving the Army. And he'd introduced her to Emily.

"Think you could look at that snowblower next?" Gunny asked.

"If I have time," she said. "I have to be at Gunny's Watering Hole in an hour." JoJo engaged the parking brake, left the tractor running and climbed down. She faced Gunny and grinned. "Expecting snow?"

"We're in the Rockies. You never know when it's gonna snow. It could snow in the middle of July. And we're getting close to the fall season. If you're worried about the Watering Hole," Gunny said, "I know the boss. I'm sure he'll cut you some slack over a couple of minutes." He winked.

JoJo's lips twisted. "The boss might excuse me a few minutes, but his daughter RJ isn't due back from picking up supplies in Colorado Springs for another hour and a half."

"I'm sure I could get Jake or Max to help me with the lunch crowd."

"I don't like to rely on the Brotherhood Protectors to wait tables at the bar. I'm sure they have better things to do," JoJo said.

"Not while they're in between assignments. That was the deal when they set up shop on the ranch.

They promised to help out here in between assignments."

Truth was, JoJo wasn't really comfortable yet with the men who were setting up a Brotherhood Protectors Colorado office at the Lost Valley Ranch, although they'd done nothing to make her feel uncomfortable. In fact, they'd saved RJ's life. Now, RJ was head over heels for Jake Cogburn.

RJ had been so infatuated with the man that she'd wanted JoJo to try dating again, going so far as to set her up with Max Thornton for the Sadie Hawkins Day dance, which had been entirely too awkward for JoJo's liking. She almost felt sorry for the guy. Every time he'd touched her, she'd jumped. It wasn't until he'd taken her into his arms and danced a very slow dance that she'd finally relaxed with him.

He'd barely spoken two words to her all evening. Fortunately, the slow dance had been really slow. The man had a limp and didn't move around as fast. She would've told him no on the dance, but she'd kind of felt bad for him because he had that limp. She hadn't wanted him to think she was too embarrassed to be seen dancing with someone with a limp.

Later, she'd seen the irony in it. He'd probably asked her to dance thinking she'd wanted to, and he hadn't wanted to disappoint her, and she hadn't wanted to turn him down in case it would make him feel like his limp was keeping her from dancing with him. She chuckled. If they'd only been open and honest with one another, they could've avoided the dance altogether. But they had danced, and it had left her even more conflicted. She only knew one thing for certain, and that was she wasn't ready for a relationship.

JoJo hated that she still felt very broken. She wanted to be fixed, but she didn't see that happening until the man who had done this to her was caught. She'd even gone so far as to agree with Emily to try some hypnosis to see if it could bring back her memories. The sooner the better.

Gunny climbed on the tractor and drove it out of the barn.

JoJo worked on the snowblower for the next hour, lost in the mechanics. At least with the machines, she didn't have to carry on a conversation. It was bad enough her thoughts never stopped rolling around in her head. Too often she came back to that memory of waking up with her cheek on the dirt, her body bruised, her throat sore from having been choked. Whoever had attacked her had beaten her, raped her and buried her in the desert, thinking she'd died. JoJo had to believe that she was still left on earth for a reason. The reason was to get the person who'd done this to her. The last memory she'd had before waking in the desert, was walking to the shower tent after working in the motor pool late into the night. She had to have seen his face. If only she could remember.

Fortunately, the sun was shining through the door of the barn, giving her just enough light that she could see what she was doing. She had ruled out all the usual suspects on the engine before she tore down half of it and found the issue. Now that it was fixed, she'd reassembled the part, filled the oil reservoir and poured gasoline into the tank. When she started the engine, it roared to life.

She bent over the engine to adjust the idle when a shadow fell over her. Her heart stopped, and her breath caught in her lungs.

When a hand touched her shoulder, she reacted. JoJo grabbed the arm, bent over and flipped the man over her back. Before she could let go of his arm, he yanked her down on top of him, rolled her over and pinned her to the ground.

She fought hard, kicking, flailing, biting, everything she could to get free.

"Ouch!" The man swore.

She couldn't hear what else he said for the pounding in her ears.

"Be still, dammit." Finally, he straddled her. After pinning her arms to the ground, he leaned back far enough that the sunlight filtered through the barn door onto his face.

"JoJo," he said, "I'm not going to hurt you."

She writhed beneath him and finally looked up into his eyes. Just because she knew him didn't mean she trusted him. Her pulse still pounded. Her breathing came in ragged pants. "Get off me."

Still, he held onto her hands. "I'll let you up when you promise not to hit, scratch or bite me."

"Let me up," she said, breathing hard.

"Promise?"

"Dammit." She bucked her hips and stomped her feet on the ground, but she was well and truly trapped. "Fine. I promise."

He released her hands and rocked over to the side, jumping to his feet and out of her way.

JoJo rolled over and scrambled to her feet. She moved several steps away from him in a crouching, ready stance. Ready to take off if he should come after her, or to defend herself if he attacked her.

He held up his hands as if in surrender. "Look, I'm sorry I startled you, but you couldn't hear me over the engine."

"What do you want?" she demanded.

His lips twisted into a wry grin. "I only came to tell you that Gunny's swamped in the Watering Hole and needs your help." He dropped his hands, and then rubbed his arm where she'd bitten him.

JoJo's head spun, and her stomach roiled. She had to find a place to sit quick or she'd fall or throw up. Either way, she'd make more of an ass of herself than she already had with this man. She spied an over-turned five-gallon bucket, sat down on it and put her head between her knees.

"Are you okay?" Careful to stay out of her range, he squatted beside her.

"I'm fine," she said. "Just don't…"

"Don't touch you?" he asked. And he chuckled. "Trust me, I promise not to touch you unless you want me to."

Her heart beat fast, and her head still spun. Gray fog moved in, and JoJo felt herself tip over on the bucket.

"Sorry," he said, as he dove to catch her, "I have to break my promise."

JoJo fought the haze sucking her down, and through that haze, she realized that Max was easing her to the ground and then removing his hands from her body.

"Hey, Tiger, talk to me," his said, his voice sounding like he was in a long tunnel. "What's wrong? Talk to me. Do I need to call an ambulance?"

"No," she said shaking her head from side to side. "I'm okay."

"You don't look so okay," he said. "You're kind of pale and pasty."

"No, really. I'm okay," she said, pushed the hair out of her face and tried to sit up. Her vision blurred, and she lay back.

"Let me help you sit up," he said and held out his hand.

She looked at it for a moment, and then reached out and placed hers in his.

He gently pulled her up into a sitting position. "Now, you want to tell me what that was all about?"

She shook her head. "Nothing."

His eyes narrowed, and he stared into hers.

Heat rose into her cheeks. "It's not any of your business."

His lips twitched in the hint of a smile. "It is when I'm thrown, kicked and bitten."

She glanced away from his face. "It's not something I want to talk about."

Max's brow furrowed as he continued to stare at her. Finally, he sighed. "At least, let me get you up to the lodge."

"No," she shook her head, "I need to help Gunny."

"Let me get you up to the lodge, and *I'll* go help Gunny."

She shook her head, her lips pressing together. "He wouldn't have asked you to come get me if he didn't need me."

He gave her a crooked smile. "True, I'm not as fast as you are delivering trays to tables. I might have dropped a few glasses on the floor. Gunny muttered something like, 'Snowblower be damned. Go get her.'" His grin broadened.

"Sorry. I should've skipped fixing the snowblower and come to work at the bar."

"It's okay," Max said. "I know my limitations. It didn't hurt my feelings."

"I just need to get on my feet, and then I'll be all

right." Though her head had stopped spinning, JoJo wasn't positive her legs would hold her if she stood.

"Seriously," Max said, "you need to go up to the lodge and lie down for a little bit."

Ignoring him, she bunched her legs beneath her and pushed to her feet.

When she swayed, he reached out and cupped her elbow. "Again, I broke my promise, but I didn't want you to fall."

She leaned into his grip until her body quit swaying and her head cleared. "I'm feeling better already," she said though she felt sick to her stomach. Why did she have to be this way? Why couldn't she act like a normal person, instead of flipping her shit when somebody came up behind her? Add the fact she'd told Max never to touch her again, and then he'd had to touch her to keep her from falling all over the floor. Heat burned in her cheeks. She squared her shoulders and faced him. "I'm really sorry if I hurt you."

His mouth quirked up on one side. "It wasn't something I was expecting, but I'll survive. Now, which direction are you going? To the lodge or to the Watering Hole?"

She gave him a tight smile. "The Watering Hole."

"Okay then, I'm going with you."

"That won't be necessary," she said. "I'll get there on my own."

"I'd rather you didn't. Not a choice," he said. "I

promise not to touch you this time, unless you fall again."

A flash of guilt filled her. The man had taken care of her when she'd more or less attacked him. "I'm sorry. Thank you for looking after me." She went to the hose outside the barn and washed her hands, getting some of the grease off before she walked to the Watering Hole where she would scrub her hands with a strong soap.

Max walked alongside her, his limp more pronounced than before.

JoJo grimaced. "Did I hurt your leg when I threw you?"

"Don't worry about it. Sometimes, I just have to work out the kinks."

"Do you mind if I asked what happened? I mean, you were active duty at one point. Did you get injured in the war?"

His lips firmed into a thin line.

"Hey," she said, "if you don't want to talk about it, that's fine with me."

He shook his head. "No, it's okay. I deployed five times. Five times, I came back intact with no major injuries. It was just my lucky day when I got this." He tapped his leg.

"How so?" she asked.

"I was in charge of mountain training. We were rappelling on a cliff. I'd done it maybe a hundred times before, no problems. Just happened to be that day something went wrong, my D-ring broke, and I fell two-hundred-fifty-feet to the ground."

JoJo shot a startled look toward him. "Oh my God, that's awful. How can you call that your lucky day?"

He gave her a slow smile. "Though I broke almost every bone in my body, I survived. I didn't have bleeding on the brain. The doctor said I was lucky I didn't die." His smile faded, and he stared off into the distance. "Sometimes, I wonder."

"For having broken every bone in your body, and you still lived to tell about it, I'd say you're doing pretty good."

"I suppose. It's hard to start over when all you've known is the Army."

JoJo nodded. "I know exactly what you mean. I enlisted straight out of high school. Coming off active duty and trying to assimilate into civilian society has been a challenge," she said. "I may not have been shot at as many times as you were. But deployments were..." She waved a hand.

"Intense?"

Her eyes widened. "Exactly. Then you get back to the real world—as some people consider it—and there's no sense of life and death or urgency whatsoever."

"Now, you know everything there is to know about me," Max said. "I'm a broken-down soldier who's trying to figure out his way in life again. If it weren't for the Brotherhood Protectors, I'd still be looking for a job. When my only skills include weaponry, tactics and mountaineering, my resume doesn't check a lot of employers' boxes."

"Sounds like the Brotherhood Protectors have got your number though," JoJo said. "From what RJ tells me, they've done good things up in Montana, and now, they are looking to do that here in Colorado. So, you'll be on the ground floor of this new office. That has to be a good thing."

He nodded. "We're still in the startup phase. Word hasn't gotten out, so I still don't have my first assignment. On the other hand, it's nice that we can help with the remodeling and also help Gunny manage the dude ranch and bar."

"And it's a good thing the Brotherhood Protectors came along when they did," JoJo said. "The rent you guys are paying on the place has really helped out Gunny."

When they reached the back of the Watering Hole bar, Max opened the door for her and held it, waiting for her to go in.

She paused and met his gaze. "Again, I'm sorry I attacked you, and thank you for coming to my rescue when I passed out."

He nodded. "My pleasure. And you didn't hurt me, except for the part where you bit me. No worries, and maybe, someday, you'll be comfortable enough to tell me what happened today. What scared you so much you felt the need to deep six me."

Or not, JoJo thought, as she entered the building. Being raped and almost killed was not something she felt she could share with any man at that point. Not even Gunny.

CHAPTER 2

BANISHED from waiting tables in the bar, Max helped Gunny make sandwiches in the kitchen while RJ and JoJo handled the bar and dining area in the Watering Hole.

"Thanks for helping out in the kitchen." Gunny swiped a slice of bread with a layer of mayo and slapped it onto the other side of the sandwich.

"I'm sorry I wasn't more help in the dining area," Max said. "My leg's still a little stiff and makes for an unsteady gait."

Gunny nodded, cut the roast beef sandwich in half and laid it onto a plate. "While you're still renovating, recruiting and getting the word out that Brotherhood Protectors are here in Colorado, I'm really appreciative of all the help the organization is giving us here at the Lost Valley Ranch."

Max nodded. "We're more than happy to help. I

don't know about Jake, but I'd go crazy if I didn't have anything to do."

Gunny grinned. "There's always something to do on the ranch, and if not on the ranch, then here in the Watering Hole. Speaking of something to do," Gunny said, "I haven't even told RJ yet, but I had a local politician schedule a retreat for this weekend."

"That's only four days away," Max said.

Gunny grimaced. "Less than that. The politician and his aide will be here tomorrow. The rest of his campaign committee will be here on Thursday."

Max hiked an eyebrow. "That soon?"

With a nod, Gunny pulled out a hamburger bun and scooped a burger off the grill, sliding it onto the bun. The man didn't seem in the least stressed. "That soon."

"Are you ready?" Max plucked a leaf of lettuce from the head sitting beside the old Marine and laid it on the plate beside the hamburger.

"Considering it's kind of late in the season and schools are all back in session, we can use the business, and I didn't have any reservations tying up the conference room. So, the timing's good." He glanced up. "I'm just looking forward to a little help taking care of all the people who will be here. Some will be here for the weekend, and some will just be commuting back and forth from Colorado Springs. They're gearing up for the next election. So, it'll be a mix of campaign staff, and they'll also have a meet-

and-greet or a shake-and-grin, or whatever civilians call it, for the locals to come out to the ranch and get to know the candidate."

Max cut into a tomato and placed a slice on the plate with the hamburger. "Sounds kind of like a big deal to me."

Gunny shrugged. "We'll have a big barbecue on Friday night and invite the public. Saturday will be an ATV tour. We'll take the campaign staff out for little teambuilding activities, so they can get to know each other and have a little fun together. Thankfully, they'll be in town Saturday night at a restaurant that they've reserved in Fool's Gold. I'll have RJ and JoJo working pretty much 24/7. They'll be on call for whatever the guests might need, along with me."

"Any way that I can help, count me in," Max said. He scooped fries onto the plate and set it on the window ledge between the kitchen and the bar.

Gunny leaned toward the window and shouted, "Order up!"

The man was a rock. Nothing ruffled him. Not even the thought of a crowd of people showing up with only a day or two to prepare.

"Seems like there will be a lot of work getting ready for this."

"It'll get done," Gunny said with confidence. "I have a chuckwagon stored in a shed that I'll pull out for the Friday night barbecue. It has a huge grill on one side and drink chests on the other. We'll have ranch activities for all the guests. RJ and JoJo will conduct the ATV tour Saturday."

"Sounds like fun," Max said.

"I just hope the weather cooperates," Gunny said. "There's supposed to be an early cold front sweeping down from the north late Friday evening, hopefully, after the barbecue."

"If it's cold, will they still go out on the ATVs?" Max asked.

"It'll be up to our guests. We do have coveralls we use during the winter for our snowmobile rides. We can still do ATV rides when it's cold as long as everyone wears the coveralls."

"You know I trained in mountaineering. We're familiar with snowmobiles and ATVs getting around in the mountains. And also, I'm also experienced in rappelling and actual mountain climbing," Max said. "Not that I do too much of that anymore." He touched his leg.

"I'll keep that in mind," Gunny said. "I don't want to abuse the Brotherhood Protectors' offer to help, but it sure will be nice that you guys are here and that, if you're not busy, you could help."

Max grinned. "It's a good thing the renovations are nearing a close. It's looking pretty good in the basement of the lodge."

Gunny nodded. "I was surprised at how modern and up to date all the equipment is down there and yet how rustic the décor is. I heard

Kujo and Jake talking about the design before Kujo headed back to Montana and his pregnant wife."

"Hank Patterson wanted to make sure that, if things didn't work out with an office for the Brotherhood Protectors in Colorado, that he left you with something you could use. A pristine white basement wasn't in keeping with Lost Valley Ranch's Old West theme."

Gunny nodded. "And I appreciate that, although any improvement would be better than what was there before. Nothing but the best for Hank Patterson. Business must be good up there in Montana. I've heard only good things about the Brotherhood Protectors and what they're doing for people who need help."

Max nodded. He'd checked into Hank's organization before agreeing to come on board. "I'm looking forward to my first assignment, and I hope that I can do the Brotherhood proud."

"I'm sure you will. Looks to me like Hank Patterson's got an eye for good people. We were sure glad to get Jake here. If it weren't for him, our RJ wouldn't be with us anymore."

At that moment, RJ pushed the swinging door into the kitchen. "We could use some food for these hungry folks." She spied the plates and grinned. "Oh, good. The sandwiches are ready." She loaded them onto a large round tray and looked at Max and

Gunny, her eyes narrowing. "What are you two talking about."

Max let Gunny answer.

"Nothing but a pretty big gig coming this weekend." Gunny didn't look up as he spoke.

About to turn with the tray in her arms, RJ froze, her eyes widening. "What did you say?"

"We got a big gig for this weekend." This time, Gunny looked up, a smile tugging at the corners of his lips.

"Gig? We're not a rock band." She glared at her father. "Explain."

"Gonna fill the rooms, throw a big party and entertain a pile of people Thursday to Sunday when they check out."

"You're kidding, right?" She shifted the weight of the tray in her arms. "Is that why you had me get all those supplies?"

Gunny nodded. "They faxed over a contract today while you were down in Colorado Springs picking up all those supplies."

"Wasn't that putting the cart before the horse?" RJ asked.

"I already had the check. I just didn't want to say anything until I had the contract in hand, but now that I do, you've already purchased all the supplies."

"Holy hell, Gunny." RJ rolled her eyes. "Who are we hosting?"

"We have a politician's campaign staff showing up

this weekend for a retreat and a public barbecue to introduce the candidate to the locals and give them a chance to shake and grin."

RJ plunked the heavy tray of food down on the counter. "We're doing what this weekend?"

"I know it's short notice," Gunny said. "But with it being so late in the season, we only had two reservations for lodging this weekend, and I thought, what the hell? We can do this."

"Why the heck didn't you tell me earlier?" RJ threw her hands in the air. "Like before I went to get all the supplies?"

Max almost laughed at how worked up RJ was and how calm Gunny remained.

The old Marine went back to making sandwiches, his focus on his hands, not his daughter's wrath. "I didn't want you to get all anxious and riled before you drove into Colorado Springs."

RJ spun away from the tray, walked a few steps and spun back. "Are you kidding me? We only have a couple days to pull this thing together."

Gunny grimaced. "Uh, actually, we have until tomorrow."

"Tomorrow?" RJ's eyes widened. "Tomorrow! They're getting here tomorrow?" She turned, paced away and returned. "How are we supposed to get ready for all that by tomorrow?"

"Don't worry about it. There's only gonna be two

for tomorrow. The candidate and his executive officer are coming in early."

"Again, how are we supposed to get everything ready by tomorrow even if it's just two of them?"

"Two people won't be a big deal," Gunny assured her. "We have enough rooms empty, and they're all clean. We're only providing breakfast. They'll take care of themselves for lunch and dinner. They want to scout out what's available in Fool's Gold, and they want to check out the casino." Gunny nodded toward the tray of food. "You need to get that food out to those people. There's some hungry guys out there."

RJ planted her fists on her hips. "As far as I'm concerned, we should shut down the Watering Hole for the rest of the day."

Gunny shook his head. "I'm not going to do that. We'll be fine. We have everything ready as we do every day of the week."

"We haven't used the conference room in a month. It probably has a layer of dust and needs to have tables and chairs set out to accommodate whatever the guests might need. And a public barbecue will take a lot more planning than just a few days. I don't think we bought nearly enough food to feed who knows how many people might show up."

"I ordered plenty of food, and we have enough paper plates to feed an army." He sliced a club sandwich in half and laid the two halves on a plate. "And I had you pick up enough trash bags to clean up after that army."

"I don't know," she said. "We haven't had this big an event here since…well, since I can't remember."

JoJo stuck her head through the swinging door. "Got some hungry guys out here. Are you gonna bring those plates out, or do you need me to take them? And I need you back behind the bar, RJ. Got an order for two bottles of Guinness, a double whiskey on the rocks and ginger ale for the designated driver."

"Got it. I'll be right out. Wait, JoJo. Did you know that we're having a big public barbecue on Friday, and that we're hosting a politician and his campaign staff for the rest of the week?"

JoJo nodded. "Yeah, and you and I are taking the campaign staff on an ATV tour on Saturday."

"What?" RJ said.

"Here, let me get that tray." JoJo crossed the kitchen floor, scooped up the tray, balanced it on her shoulder and pushed through the swinging door out into the dining room.

RJ planted a fist on her hips. "Why is it I'm the last one to know?"

Gunny grinned. "Sometimes, you just get a little bit too wound up with planning, girl. Besides, you operate better under pressure."

Max had to clamp down hard on his teeth to keep from smiling at the look of disgust on RJ's face.

"What would you do if I walked out of here right now and quit?" she demanded.

Gunny grinned. "You won't. You love me too much."

She glared at her father for another second, and then the frown slipped, and her forehead smoothed. "It's a damn good thing I do love you. I also know why you haven't remarried since Mama died. No other woman would put up with this."

Gunny wadded up a dish towel and threw it at RJ. "Go back to work, girl."

RJ gave her father a stern look. "We're talking later."

"I'd planned on it. I thought we'd talk through the event at dinner and lay out plans."

RJ pointed a finger at her father. "I'm taking away your phone privileges."

"Ha," he said.

RJ spun and left the room.

Max chuckled. "You two have a special relationship."

Gunny's grin faded. "Yes, we do. I love my daughter more than life itself, but there are days when she looks so much like her mother that it hurts. After her mother died, I didn't think I could love anyone as much as RJ. Then JoJo came along. She's like a second daughter to me. I love that little spitfire and would hate to see anyone hurt her."

"The two of them are very capable young women. I know they make you proud."

Gunny nodded, and then pinned Max with a hard stare. "You two seemed to have hit it off at the Sadie Hawkins dance the other night."

Max's brow dipped. "I don't know about hit it off. I might have stepped on her toes a couple times during the dance. She doesn't seem too interested. In fact, I'd said she's a little skittish around men." Max rubbed the back of his head where a knot was forming from his altercation with the feisty JoJo.

"That JoJo. Something bad happened to her while she was on active duty." Gunny's lips pressed together. "She won't talk about it. While she was deployed, she used to call often, whenever she could get internet access. Then she went a couple weeks without contact. I was getting worried. I was about to call the Red Cross to see if they could get in touch with her unit and find out what was going on. I tried text messaging her. I tried e-mailing her, even RJ tried both and nothing. And then we got a call from a doctor at Ramstein Air Force Base, Germany. He said that one of his patients wanted to talk to me and RJ. She had been in the hospital, and we didn't even know it. Because we weren't family, they wouldn't release any of the details to us. All we were told was that she had sustained a head injury, and she might have some troubles with her memory, but that she'd remembered enough to call us when she came to."

Max's chest tightened.

"They medically discharged her from the Army with TBI, traumatic brain injury. When they shipped her home, we picked her up from the airport. We're pretty much the only family she has. Her father deserted her family when she was just a baby. Her mother died before she graduated from high school." Gunny shook his head. "Why she entered the Army, I don't know. She should have gone into the Marines."

Max scowled. "Hey."

He held up his hands. "No offense."

"None taken."

"You damn Army pukes are too sensitive." Gunny grinned. "But you make one hell of a sandwich. Why don't you take those two plates out to JoJo and let her serve her customers? Maybe if you talk to her enough, she'll open up about what happened to her. She sure hasn't opened up to me or to RJ, but she's seeing a friend of ours at the VA Hospital. A therapist. I really hope it helps. In the meantime, go easy on her. She must have gone through hell."

Max scooped up the plates of sandwiches and carried them out to the dining room, almost bumping into JoJo who was heading into the kitchen.

"Oh good," she said. "I was looking for those." When she took the sandwiches from his hands, their fingers touched.

A jolt of electricity shot up his arms and spread warmth throughout his chest.

JoJo's eyes widened, and her pupils flared. If Max hadn't still been holding onto the plates, she would've dropped them. Her hands fell to her sides.

"Are you okay?" Max asked.

She looked down at her hands, and then back up at him. "I—I'm fine." Then she carefully took the plates from his hands without touching his fingers, turned and hurried away without another word.

"Max," RJ called out, "can you carry this tray of drinks over to table five?"

"Are you sure you want me to?" he asked.

RJ grinned. "It takes practice."

He shook his head. "It'll be your loss if it all ends up on the floor."

"I'll take my chances," she said. "You've got this."

He lifted the heavy tray off the counter and limped across the room to table five, proud of himself when he delivered the drinks without spilling the contents, dropping the tray or making an idiot of himself.

JoJo collected empties off a table with five rowdy men seated around it. Just when she laid the last bottle on the tray and was about to pick it up, a big, booted foot swept out and clipped her ankle. JoJo toppled onto one of the men's laps.

"Hey, JoJo, didn't know you cared," the man with the big foot said. "Come give ol' Roy some sugar."

Max stiffened as JoJo's eyes widened, and her face blanched white. "Let me up," she said. "Let me up."

She struggled against the meaty hands holding her down.

Roy wrapped his arms around her and held her tightly. "Hey, sweetheart, all I want's a little sugar."

Max flew across the room, yanked the man's hands away from JoJo and pulled her off his lap. He let go of her immediately, and she ran past the bar through the swinging door and into the kitchen. And from the way a door slammed in the kitchen, she was headed out the back exit.

Max pointed to the man seated in the chair. "Out."

Roy's eyebrows rose. "What? I didn't do nothin'. She fell into my lap."

"The hell she did." Max glared at the man. "You tripped her and made her fall into your lap. Get out."

The man pushed to his feet. He must have been at least six-feet-seven. He towered over Max's six-feet-three inches and weighed at least twice as much as Max.

Max didn't give a rat's ass how big the guy was. The man had been an asshole to JoJo. Max pushed his shoulders back and squared off with Roy. He wasn't backing down.

Roy's lip curled up on one corner. "You gonna make me leave?"

Max's eyes narrowed. "If I have to."

"You and what army?" he sneered.

"I don't need anybody else. I *am* the Army."

"And if he needs any more help, he has the

Marines with him," Gunny said beside him. "Get out, Roy."

"And I'm the Marines' back-up." RJ appeared beside Gunny, carrying a shotgun.

Roy eyed the shotgun. "I'll bet you don't even know how to shoot that."

Gunny's bark of laughter made all the heads turn in the dining room. "Then you don't know my daughter. She's a better shot than I ever dreamed of being. And I was a sniper. A damn good one. You telling me you want to test her skills?"

Roy stood for another second or two, and then shook his head. "I don't have to take this crap from anybody, and the food wasn't that great either. I ain't payin' for it." He turned and pushed past Gunny and stalked out the front door of the bar. The men sitting at the table all looked away, their cheeks red.

"Sorry about that, Gunny. Didn't know he was going to be such a jerk," one of them said. He threw a couple of twenties on the table. "That should cover his and ours. Don't worry. We won't bring him back again."

"Good, because he's not welcome here. Thank you for understanding." Gunny smiled. "Stay for a while. Have a drink on the house."

The man grinned. "Thanks, Gunny."

Gunny turned to RJ, meeting her gaze.

RJ nodded. "I'll go check on her."

Max wanted to go with RJ to find JoJo. He was

worried about her. He suspected whatever had happened to her had to do with men, and that would explain why she'd flipped him in the barn and lost it when Roy grabbed her.

"Think you could handle making sandwiches?" Gunny asked.

Max nodded. "I think I can figure that out."

"Good." Gunny grabbed the tray full of empty mugs. "I'll take care of the bar and wait the tables."

Max wished that Jake hadn't gone into Colorado Springs to talk with contractors about the renovation plans. They could sure use his help now.

Soon enough, the lunch crowd thinned. Eventually all of them left. Max helped Gunny clean the tables, the floors and the kitchen before he headed for the lodge. He found himself looking for JoJo, skipping the lodge and going out to the barn. As he approached the door to the barn, he whistled a tune just to make sure she knew someone was coming. He met RJ coming out as he entered the barn.

RJ shook her head. "I wouldn't go in. I think she needs some time alone."

Max wanted to go in and at least talk to JoJo. He wanted to tell her that things had worked out and the guy had left, but he took RJ's advice and didn't go inside. Instead, he leaned against the door all casual like and stared into the shadowy interior of the barn.

JoJo was on her knees beside an ATV, tinkering with the engine.

"Do you go out on the ATVs much?" he asked.

For a long moment she didn't respond, but her hand stilled on the socket wrench she was holding. Then she quickly tightened a bolt. When she finished, she pushed to her feet and turned to face him. "Yes, I've been out on the ATVs a lot since I've been here. Don't you have anything better to do than lurk around the barn?"

He chuckled. "I was hoping you'd give me a lesson on that move you performed on me that flipped me over your back and landed me on mine."

Her eyes narrowed. "I'm betting you know a few of your own."

"I do," he said, dipping his head. "But I was impressed with yours."

"I can give you the number of the woman who taught it to me."

"I'd appreciate that." Still leaning against the door, he tipped his head toward the ATV. "I wouldn't mind taking one of these for a spin."

JoJo wiped her hands on a rag. "I'm sure Gunny wouldn't mind if you took one out."

"I don't suppose you have a map of the trails out here, do you?"

She shook her head. "Now, I suppose you're gonna ask me if I'd take you out and show you the trails?"

He grinned. "That would be nice, but I can ask RJ if you'd rather not."

Her lips twisted. "I guess I could tomorrow. I need to plan a route for the ATV tour on Saturday."

"And I'd love to go along for the ride."

She nodded. "I suppose I owe it to you after I flipped you."

Max rubbed the back of his neck. "You really don't owe me anything, but I would appreciate it if you'd take me along for the ride."

She walked past him out into the sunshine. "Tomorrow morning. Ten o'clock." She kept walking, heading for the lodge.

Max gave her the space she needed and didn't follow until a few minutes later. He was sure he'd see her again that night at the Watering Hole, if it was as busy as it was today with the lunch crowd. They could use all the help they could get to take care of the patrons.

He watched as JoJo climbed the steps and entered the lodge. Max liked how fierce she was, and he found himself looking forward to every time he saw her.

CHAPTER 3

"ANYBODY ELSE NEED COFFEE?" RJ asked from the swinging door of the kitchen in the lodge.

JoJo raised a hand. "I'll take some but let me come help."

"I'd like some coffee, but I don't mind making it." Max started toward the kitchen.

"You can make it next time," RJ said. "I haven't had a chance to talk with JoJo all day."

Max nodded and turned back to Jake.

Gunny entered the dining room as JoJo reached the swinging door to the kitchen. "Oh good, we're all here. We can start our meeting."

"Give us a second, Gunny," RJ said. "We'll be right back with coffee."

"Let me make the coffee," Gunny said.

"Good grief." RJ rolled her eyes. "With everyone

offering to make coffee, I'm beginning to think you don't like the way I make it."

"On the contrary," Gunny said, "you make a better cup of coffee than I've ever managed."

"In that case, we've got this," RJ said. "Come on, JoJo."

JoJo chuckled and followed RJ into the kitchen.

"So, tell me what's been going on today. What have I missed?" RJ poured water into the coffeemaker and scooped grinds into the filter.

"Same old, same old," JoJo said. "Got the tractor running, and the snowblower now works. Although why we should care about the snow, I don't know. It's still fall, and the temperatures haven't gotten below forty at night."

"It's a little different up here in the mountains than it is in Colorado Springs," RJ said. "We get snow here sooner than they do in the Springs. I've known it to snow in July."

"I'd believe it," JoJo said. "It gets really cold up here at night."

"Thanks for getting the machinery up and running. What I really want to know is how are you?"

JoJo nodded. "I'm okay."

RJ faced her, a frown puckering her brow. "Look, JoJo, I'm sorry about what happened with Roy. You know you can file charges against him, don't you?"

"I don't think I'll have any more problems with

him," JoJo said. "From what Gunny said, he's not welcome at the Watering Hole anymore."

"How are your sessions going with Emily?" RJ asked.

JoJo shrugged. "About the same."

RJ shot her a twisted smile as she pulled cups out of the cabinet. "That tells me a lot."

"It's not something I like to talk about."

RJ pressed her lips together. "I've been your friend for a long time. You can tell me anything. I won't judge, and I'm a pretty good listener."

JoJo crossed the room and hugged her friend. "I know that, and I hope someday that I can talk to you about this. It's just not today."

RJ squeezed her friend hard. "I know you're hurting. When you hurt, I hurt. Something happened while you were in Afghanistan, and I wished the hell I knew what it was. But if you're not ready to talk about it, I'll respect your wishes."

"Thank you, RJ."

RJ set her at arm's length. "You know I love you. You're the sister I always wanted."

"And Gunny's like a father to me," JoJo said. "Without you two, I don't know what I would've done when I came off active duty."

"You're still welcome to move into the lodge with us." RJ stared down at her friend. "I really wish you would."

JoJo stood back and nodded. "I know. I'm just not ready, and I don't want to bring my troubles to you."

"You know we'd do anything for you," RJ insisted. "Slay dragons...throw bullies out of the bar...you know. Anything."

JoJo gave a crooked smile. "I know, and I would do the same for you." She drew in a deep breath and let it out. Then she pasted a smile on her face. "Let's talk about something else, like how we're going to support the event this politician wants to throw this weekend."

"That's why Gunny's got us all gathered—so we can work out some of the details," RJ said. "I can't believe he didn't tell me. I'm sure there were other supplies I could've picked up while I was in the Springs." RJ smiled. "Although I'm sure, if I asked, Jake would run in and find what we need. He's always going back and forth. I think he's got a new lead on a guy they want to hire for the Brotherhood Protectors."

JoJo's brow twisted. "Seems like they'd want work before they started hiring more people."

"His boss, Hank, thinks it's only a matter of time before they're inundated with work." RJ sighed. "I hope so, because I'd like to see them stay."

JoJo grinned. "You kind of like that guy, don't you?"

RJ chuckled. "Look at me, the consummate tomboy in love for the first time in her life."

"Jake's a good man," JoJo said. "You could do a lot worse."

"Sometimes, he doesn't know just how good he is. It took me a lot of convincing to get him to believe that he's not less of a man because he's one leg short."

"He gets around just fine on his prosthetic," JoJo said.

"Yes, he does." RJ's grin widened. "And missing a leg doesn't affect him one bit in the bed." Her cheeks turned a pretty shade of pink. "Who knew I'd like sex so much? It really makes a difference when you have the right partner."

JoJo turned away under the pretense of filling the sugar bowl and placing it on the tray. When she turned around, RJ had a smirk on her face.

"I saw Max come to your rescue today. So, how's it going with Max since the Sadie Hawkins dance?"

JoJo lifted a shoulder, heat rising in her cheeks. "He's a nice man, but I'm just not interested right now."

RJ frowned. "I thought you two were hitting it off. I don't think there was a hair's breadth between the two of you when you danced. A lot of belly rubbing was going on there."

JoJo's cheeks flamed. "It was just a dance."

"Some people say dancing is like having sex with your clothes on." RJ grinned. "With the right partner, of course."

JoJo snapped the lid back on the sugar canister. "It

was just a dance. I'm not interested in Max. I'm not interested in anybody. I just want to do my job and go home at night to watch my favorite game shows."

RJ snorted. "Like you watch game shows."

JoJo didn't watch game shows. She barely watched TV. Mostly, she worked out, building her muscles and her strength so that she'd never be in another position where she could be overpowered by a man and unable to defend herself. Though she felt bad about flipping Max earlier that day, she was also proud of herself. Her training had worked. Well, mostly. He had rolled her over and trapped her beneath him.

"All right," RJ said, "we won't talk about Max yet. Such a shame though. He seems to be a really nice man, and he was quick to defend you when Roy was an asshole." She held up a hand when JoJo opened her mouth to say something. "But I promise not to talk about him anymore."

JoJo shook her head. RJ would find another way. The woman was persistent in her desire to see JoJo happy.

"Come on. Let's take this coffee out to the men, and next time, we'll let them bring the coffee out to us." RJ grinned, lifted the tray and backed into the swinging door and out into the dining room.

JoJo followed. It really made her feel good to see RJ so happy.

RJ was the type of person who, if she felt content,

she wanted everybody else around her to be as content.

JoJo wanted to tell her what was going on and why she couldn't be happy. She wanted her friend to know she wouldn't be happy until she'd found the man who'd done what he had to her.

What was scary was that she'd been kidnapped from a military base and nobody knew who'd done it. There had to be a record somewhere of the vehicle that had been driven off the base and out into the desert to where she'd been buried.

Her last memory had been one of exiting the shower unit and heading toward her quarters. Everything else was a big, black, gaping hole in her memory. That was why she'd agreed to see Emily. She was hoping that by talking things out with a therapist she'd eventually remember.

Damn, she thought. She had an appointment with Emily on Thursday. With the campaign staff arriving that day, she doubted she'd be able to get away to see her, and she really wanted to. She'd call in the morning and let Emily know she wouldn't make her appointment. They'd planned on doing some hypnosis treatment. JoJo really hoped that would help unleash the memories.

"Again," Gunny was saying, "you two do not have to be involved in this event, but we could sure use the help."

Jake raised a hand. "Don't you worry about it.

We're at a standstill on the renovations, waiting for supplies to come in to do the last few things on the checklist. I want to touch base tomorrow with my new candidate to see if he's accepted our offer to come on board as a new Brotherhood Protector. Other than that, I have nothing Thursday, Friday, Saturday or Sunday. Word has yet to get out that we're here. I'm sure Hank's working on that. We won't always have this availability to assist with the lodge activities. Let us help now, while we can."

Gunny nodded and started talking about the plans he had laid out. He pressed his pen to the pad of paper in front of him and drew a timeline. "The politician, Lawrence Stover, and his aide Miles Curry, will arrive tomorrow sometime after noon. We've selected rooms for them to occupy while they're here. RJ and I will meet them and show them where to go. We'll talk them through what we've laid out and ask for any changes now, before the rest of their staff arrive. You're welcome to attend, but you don't have to. What we discuss tonight is what RJ and I will present to them tomorrow. If they have any changes, we'll let you know."

Jake, Max and JoJo nodded.

"Wednesday is Stover and Curry getting settled in and checking out the lay of the land and what they have available to them as far as conference rooms and outdoor activities go."

"You'll have to fill us in on those activities," RJ said.

Gunny nodded. "I will. They also want to go into Fool's Gold and see about arrangements they've made with the restaurant there, as well as check in with the mayor about the meet-and-greets they've scheduled. They might also make a trip out to the casino. So, Wednesday, they'll be busy with other things. We won't have to entertain them. We won't even have to provide dinner, but we will provide breakfast the next morning."

RJ and JoJo nodded.

"On Thursday, the rest of their campaign staff will arrive in the afternoon. That day, we'll provide breakfast for just the two, and we'll probably provide dinner for the team. I'll need help in the kitchen and with serving. We still have the usual patrons at the bar to take care of as well. I'm sure after dinner they'll all want to adjourn to the bar. I might suggest to them that they eat at the bar. That way I can take care of the regular patrons as well as them."

"That would work out best," Jake said. "If you have to operate both, I could work the bar while you work the lodge or vice versa."

"I'm getting better at carrying a tray, or I could make sandwiches," Max said. "I've even mixed a drink or two."

"I've been known to mix drinks as well," Jake said. "And I'm pretty handy in the kitchen."

Gunny grinned. "I appreciate it. If you two weren't here, I'd be hiring some people from Fool's Gold to come out and beef up our staff. As it is, I think I'll still hire some additional staffing. I've already put the word out for Friday night for help with serving. On Friday morning, Stover will meet with his team in the conference room, and they're going to spend the day going over his campaign strategy. All we have to do for that in the morning is make sure they have coffee and water. And I've arranged for the donut shop in town to have muffins and donuts for snacking. For lunch, we'll have them go over to the Watering Hole for sandwiches." Gunny nodded towards Max. "I could use somebody who's good at making sandwiches, Max."

Max gave him a nod. "I'll be there."

"JoJo and I will manage the bar and serve the tables," RJ said. "Unless Jake wants to mix drinks—that might help."

"Count me in," Jake said.

Gunny continued. "As soon as we're done in the Watering Hole, we'll close up for lunch early so we can get started doing the barbecue. I'll get the brisket smoking early in the morning so it will be done by the time the guests start arriving in the afternoon. We'll need to have a buffet table laid out. RJ and JoJo can help me set it up. That way, it can be self-serve, and we'll just have to keep filling the food trays. Stover has hired a band to come out to play, and they'll do their own set-up. And I've cordoned off an area of the barn. We shouldn't have to be involved in that, just keep the trash bags empty and people fed. That's the big meet and greet with the public. Got it?"

"Yes," everyone responded as one.

Gunny shot a glance toward JoJo. "Hopefully, Roy won't show up. I banned him from the Watering Hole. Maybe, he'll take that as a sign that he shouldn't show up at the lodge either."

JoJo shrugged. "Don't worry about me. If he shows up, I'll just stay away from him."

Gunny nodded. "I spoke to the sheriff today, and he said he'd be out here for the shake and grin, and he'll probably have a couple of deputies with him just to make sure nobody gets too drunk or too stupid."

JoJo admired how Gunny got everything squared away. She loved the discipline of the military. That hadn't been the reason why she'd left the Army. She had left because she hadn't felt safe within her own unit or her own people. It was one thing to have an enemy that your team pulled together to fight against. It was another to have an enemy within your own team and not know who that enemy was. She had been given the choice to return to her unit in Afghanistan or return to the States. The thought of returning to her unit had terrified her, and JoJo had never been terrified of anything.

RJ nudged JoJo with her elbow. "Hey, are you all right?" she whispered.

JoJo's mind returned to the table with four pairs of eyes on her. She gave a weak smile. "I must be tired."

"It's okay, we're almost done here," Gunny said. "Saturday, the candidate wants a team-building exercise. We're setting them up with a round robin event, taking them over to the short zipline we have, as well as the rope bridge that spans the creek."

"What about canoe races?" RJ asked.

Gunny nodded. "We'll also offer canoe races across our little lake. We'll perform those in the morning, and then we'll have an ATV tour in the afternoon."

"What about the Saturday evening meal?" JoJo asked.

Gunny shook his head. "We don't have to serve dinner that night because they have reservations in Fool's Gold at one of the local restaurants, but they will be back to sleep. And then Sunday, everyone packs up and leaves, so we only have to feed them breakfast Sunday morning."

"Sounds doable," RJ said.

"Does anyone have any questions?" Gunny asked. "I'd like for RJ and JoJo to lead the ATV tour on Saturday. RJ in front, JoJo bringing up the rear. I'd do it myself, but I still have the bar to run for lunch and dinner, and I could use some help there."

"I can stay back and help," Jake said.

Gunny nodded. "As for the zipline and the rope

bridge, I could use some help on both of those events as well. We'll do some training that morning before we invite the campaign staff out to the lake. We can divvy up the rest of the duties the morning of the events. Right now though, I need to get back to the Watering Hole. The evening crowd should be showing up around now."

"Don't you guys ever take a break?" Max asked.

"We had to keep things going to keep paying the mortgage. I have yet to adjust the hours based on the new income with the Brotherhood Protectors," Gunny said. "I'm sure it'll make the bar patrons very unhappy if I close down on any of their favorite nights of the week. I might consider hiring one more person to help staff the Watering Hole. I'm sure RJ and JoJo don't want to commit the rest of their lives to this place."

RJ stared at her father. "I've always loved the ranch. There'd have to be a really good reason to make me want to leave." Her gaze shot to Jake.

He grinned. "All the more reason to make this branch of the Brotherhood Protectors pay off," he said. "I like it here, too. Not so much for the place, but for the people running it." He reached out and took RJ's hand.

The love beaming from his eyes for RJ made JoJo's heart ache. She had dreamed of one day finding someone who'd look at her that way. But now, the only dreams she had were nightmares. She was no good to any relationship the way she was now. Which reminded her. She needed to talk to Emily and reschedule her Thursday appointment.

"I have to make a phone call, and then I'll be at the Watering Hole to help serve the dinner crowd," JoJo said.

"That's good." Gunny lifted his chin. "We all need to exchange numbers so we can communicate if need be about the event."

Each of them got out their phones and exchanged numbers amongst themselves.

"If we're done here," Gunny said, "we have more work to do at the bar."

RJ stood and glanced across at JoJo. "See you over at the Watering Hole."

JoJo nodded. "I'll be right there."

RJ turned to Jake. "If you want to join me tonight, I'll show you what drinks customers prefer for the most part and help you with any that you don't remember how to make."

He nodded. "I'm with you. Lead the way."

CHAPTER 4

AFTER THE ROOM CLEARED, JoJo pulled out her cell-phone and hit Emily's number with a video call, knowing that she would probably still be in the office. The therapist loved to work late, catching up on her notes in each of her patient's files. She'd given JoJo her personal cellphone number, which she normally didn't do for the rest of her patients, but because JoJo and Emily were part of Gunny's family, she'd stretched that rule to include JoJo and had encouraged her to call whenever she needed someone to talk to.

JoJo appreciated the offer and tried not to take advantage of it. If JoJo cancelled now, Emily would have an opportunity to fill her appointment with somebody else.

"Hey, JoJo. How's it going?" Emily's voice sounded

on the other end of the line and her face came into view on the screen.

"Okay, I guess," she said.

"You want to talk about it?" Emily asked.

She hadn't planned on it, but since she had her on the line, she figured she'd better tell her before somebody else did about what had happened in the barn that day. "I kind of lost it today," JoJo said.

"How so?" Emily's voice was a little tighter.

"One of the new guys who's here with the Brotherhood Protectors came into the barn while I was working with some loud machinery and touched me on the shoulder. I didn't know he was there until he touched me."

"Yikes," Emily said.

JoJo winced. "Yes, yikes."

"What'd you do?"

"You know those Krav Maga lessons I've been taking?" JoJo asked.

Emily nodded. "Yes."

JoJo met Emily's gaze. "Well...they worked."

Emily chuckled. "Well, I hope you didn't break the man..."

"I flipped him over my shoulder, and he landed on his back."

"Dang, girl. I'd say the lessons worked." Emily grinned. "Bet he didn't expect it."

"No. I think he hit his head, but he seemed to be

okay. He got up and helped with the lunch crowd, so I guess he wasn't too badly injured."

"Oh my," Emily said. "How did he take it?"

"Better than I did."

"What do you mean?" Emily asked.

"After I flipped him, he spun me over and trapped me beneath him."

Emily's tone softened. "I take it you didn't like that very much."

JoJo shook her head. "No. He said he only held me down to keep me from biting, hitting, or scratching him."

"And were you doing all of that?" Emily asked, a smile playing at her lips.

JoJo's cheeks heated. "All of that."

"That's the kind of knee-jerk reaction you're going to have until you resolve these issues. Even then, you might not get rid of those urges for fight or flight."

"I'm so tired of jumping at every little thing." She waved her hand in the air as she walked across the dining room. "Emily, I flipped that man. What if it had been Gunny? I could've really hurt him."

Emily chuckled. "I'm impressed that you flipped him. At least you know that you can defend yourself."

"But I didn't," JoJo said. "He rolled me over and pinned me down. I was back in the same position where I couldn't defend myself. So, the Krav Maga lessons only worked halfway."

"Which man was it?" Emily asked.

JoJo cringed. "Max."

"The man who took you to the Sadie Hawkins dance?"

"One and the same," JoJo said. "I'm really making a great impression on him by now."

"And do you care what kind of impression you make with this particular man?"

JoJo's gut reaction was to say no, but she hesitated. "I don't want Gunny to lose business because one of his employees is attacking his guests."

"Is that the only reason why you're worried about the impression you make on this particular man?"

She'd be lying if she said yes. "I don't know," she admitted.

"Sounds like you might like this guy."

"If I did, what good is that? He's got his own issues. He doesn't need someone like me."

"Hey, JoJo, don't knock yourself. You're an amazing woman who's suffered a lot and who came through it. You have a lot to offer to any relationship. Hell, woman, you lived to tell about it."

"That's just it," JoJo said. "I didn't live to tell about it. I just lived. I can't remember enough to tell anybody about who did this to me. That man is still out there. He could be doing what he did to me to other women. You and I have tried talking about it, and it's gotten me nowhere. What else can we do?"

"We really need to try the hypnosis," Emily said.

"At this point, I'd consider voodoo or witchcraft. Anything to get those memories out of my head."

Emily laughed. "Well, I'm not qualified for either of those, but I have been known to do some hypnosis. Want to try that at your appointment on Thursday?"

JoJo sighed. "About Thursday…I have to cancel."

"Are you sure? I mean, we don't have to do the hypnosis then. We can wait for another visit."

"No, really, I need to cancel. We have a big event happening this weekend on the ranch. It's all hands on deck. I have to be here."

"Is it Lawrence Stover's big meet and greet that they're having on Friday? I saw a report on the news about it just a few minutes ago."

JoJo nodded. Politicians knew how to work the media to get the word out quickly. "That's the one, only Stover and his sidekick will be arriving tomorrow. His campaign staff arrives on Thursday. So, I need to be here."

"Understood," Emily said. "You know, I didn't schedule any appointments for Friday, and my last appointment on Thursday is around two. I could come out, and we could do the hypnosis session at the lodge."

"I'm not sure I'll have time."

"Well, I'd like to come out anyway and visit with Gunny, RJ and you. Maybe I can help with the events this weekend as well."

JoJo smiled. "Gunny would love that. I swear you're one of his favorites."

"As are you, JoJo, as are you," Emily said. "That old curmudgeon has a heart of gold."

"He does. And he collects strays," JoJo added.

Emily laughed. "And I'm grateful for that. I wouldn't be the therapist I am today without his help."

"And I wouldn't be able to put a roof over my head without the job he gave me."

"You know he'd put you up at the lodge."

JoJo smiled. "I know, and he keeps asking when I'm moving in, but for now with my nightmares...it's best that I'm in my own apartment. That way I don't disturb him, RJ, or their guests."

"That's a good point, but then you also don't have the support handy when you do have those terrible nightmares."

"They're mine," JoJo said. "I don't want the others to be involved in them."

"Ever heard that phrase, no man is an island?" Emily asked.

"Yeah, so?"

"That goes for women too. RJ and Gunny are family. They'd happily help share your burden."

"Are you trying to get rid of me?" JoJo asked.

Emily chuckled. "Not at all. I just want to help make you whole again. I didn't know you before, but I can guess you're only half the person you used to be…walking in shadows, afraid of the dark. RJ and Gunny have enough love in their hearts to help chase away those shadows."

"I know," JoJo said. "And Gunny helped by putting me through Krav Maga lessons, and not a day goes by that RJ doesn't ask for me to open up and tell her what's wrong."

"You're not ready, are you?" Emily said.

"No, it's still too raw. And though I know it wasn't my fault and I didn't ask for it, I still feel embarrassed and humiliated." JoJo's throat tightened, and tears welled in her eyes. "They found me naked and buried in the sand."

"JoJo, we all came into this world naked. Don't let that bother you. And again, it was not your fault. No woman asks to be raped, and they sure as hell don't ask to be beaten and left to die."

The love and kindness in Emily's voice hit a chord in JoJo. She took a shuddering breath and held back the tears. "The logic in me agrees with you one-hundred percent, but then there's the emotional side of me that wonders how people will look at me if they know what happened. I don't want them to think of me as dirty. And I don't want them to look at me with pity in their eyes."

"I really wish you'd consider joining the sexual violence survivor's support group. It really does help to know that you're not the only one. JoJo, you survived. Not everyone who went through what you have does. And you're worthy of love and acceptance. Join the group. It'll help."

"Again, maybe someday," JoJo whispered. "I'm just not ready."

"Neither were they," Emily said gently. "But they did it."

"So noted," JoJo said. "Now, I really have to get to work."

"And I need to wrap things up and get ready to go home," Emily sighed. "I'll see you on Thursday?"

"You bet," JoJo said. "I'll let Gunny know you're coming."

"Good, I enjoy being outdoors. I can help him do anything he needs done. I owe that man so much."

JoJo ended the call. She owed Gunny, too. He'd taken her in, no questions.

She hurried over to the Watering Hole where a crowd had already gathered, hollering for drinks and food. Hopefully, she'd get through the evening without another Roy pushing her buttons. Max would be there as well. She might even bump into him a time or two. The thought sent shivers of awareness across her body, and warmth coiled at her center. Since her rape, she hadn't wanted any man, but Max gave her a sense of hope that one day she would.

Thankfully, the regulars didn't stay past nine o'clock. They headed back to Fool's Gold or their ranches for the night since the next day would be another workday.

After they stacked the chairs, mopped the floors and cleaned the kitchen, Gunny, RJ, Jake, Max and JoJo left through the rear exit of the Watering Hole.

Jake took RJ's hand. "Feel like a cup of hot cocoa? Maybe even a foot rub?"

RJ sighed. "You are a man after my own heart."

"I certainly hope so." He raised her hand to his lips and pressed a kiss to the backs of her knuckles. "They say the way to a woman's heart is through her feet."

RJ laughed. "Whoever they are, they're right."

Jake and RJ walked away, leaning into each other and holding hands.

Once again, JoJo felt her heart ache with the sight of the love the two had found in each other.

"I'm headed to bed," Gunny said, breaking into JoJo's thoughts. "Got an early morning. Before I go, JoJo, do you want me to follow you into town and make sure Roy doesn't give you any trouble?"

JoJo shook her head. "No, I'll be fine."

Gunny nodded. "Let me know. Give me a call when you get in, so I know you got in safe."

"That won't be necessary," Max said. "I'll follow her into town and see that she makes it to her door."

JoJo frowned. "I can make it on my own. You don't need to follow me."

He shook his head. "I'm going that way anyway. I

need to stop by the grocery store and pick up a few things."

Her frown deepened. "You're not just saying that?"

He shook his head. "No, actually, I hate to admit it, but I have a sweet tooth, and I'm all out of my peppermint candies that I love. And I know that I don't need the sugar," he patted his flat stomach, "or need the calories, but life wouldn't be worth living if you couldn't indulge every once in a while."

She laughed, imagining this big Special Forces guy sucking on a peppermint candy. "Fine. You can follow me to town, but you don't have to follow me all the way to my apartment. Once we get to town, you can go off to the grocery store. It's in the opposite direction."

His lips pressed together tightly. "What kind of gentleman would I be if I didn't make sure that you made it to your door?"

JoJo cocked one eyebrow. "One that's not nearly as irritating as you are?"

He grinned. "Ha, but I think deep down you like that I'm irritating."

Her lips twisted. "It has to be because you're cute. Otherwise, people wouldn't put up with you."

His grin broadened. "Oh, so you think I'm cute?" He puffed out his chest. "And all my friends told me I had a face only a mother could love."

JoJo rolled her eyes. "Liar. You're too handsome

for your own good. Lucky you didn't land on your face in that fall."

He nodded. "Yes, I was. Fortunately, I was wearing a helmet, which probably saved my brain from being scrambled. I guess that's one more thing to be thankful for." He grinned. "Look, I promise not to walk you up to your door. However, I would like to see you make it into your apartment before I go to the grocery store."

JoJo's eyes narrowed. "Why do you care?"

"I guess I feel like I'm responsible for your well-being after rescuing you from Roy's lap." He winked. "I promise you chivalry is not dead." He raised his hands in surrender. "It's not like I'm asking for anything in return. I just want to know you're safe getting in your own apartment."

She rolled her eyes. "Fine. But I don't need somebody looking out for me. I can take care of myself."

He rubbed the back of his head. "I realize that."

Her lips twisted into a wry grin. "You're not going to let me forget that are you?"

He shook his head. "Nope. And I'm not likely to forget it either."

JoJo hit the unlock button on her car. Before she could reach for the door handle, Max was there opening the door for her. She frowned but said a grudging *thank you* as she climbed into her car and closed the door.

CHAPTER 5

MAX LIMPED TO HIS TRUCK, tired after a day on his feet. He hated that the limp was even more pronounced, and he hated that JoJo saw it. Why he should be so concerned about what she thought of him, he didn't know. He kind of liked the spitfire. She didn't take any guff from anybody, including him.

Max followed JoJo into Fool's Gold. When he was supposed to turn right to go to the grocery store, he instead turned left and followed her. After three or four blocks, she turned to the right and drove another block to a small apartment complex. He hung back, giving her room until she drove into a space in the parking lot.

When she got out of her vehicle and started up to her apartment on the second floor, Max pulled into the parking lot with the intention of turning around.

He paused and waited to see that she made it into the apartment and closed the door behind her, locking it, he hoped.

Her light came on inside.

Max sighed, backed out of the parking lot, and pulled out onto the road.

As punchy as she'd been when she'd flipped him over in the barn, he was almost certain that she had experienced some kind of attack. And based on her reaction to Roy pulling her down into his lap, she'd probably been attacked by a man.

Max pressed his foot to the accelerator, his fingers tightening on the steering wheel. As he drove away from the apartment complex, a dark, four-door sedan passed him going the opposite direction. He slowed and watched as the vehicle pulled into the parking lot. For all he knew, it could be another resident of JoJo's building.

He started to drive away, but something tugged at his gut. Instead, he circled the block and came back to the apartment complex. The dark sedan stood in the parking lot, someone still in the driver's seat. He'd backed into a position across from JoJo's door.

Max frowned. He took another turn around the block and came back.

The same vehicle remained, the driver still behind the wheel. Granted, he could be on the phone talking to someone and didn't want to get out until he ended the conversation. But why had he backed into the parking place, and why was he sitting right across from JoJo's door?

Max didn't think it was Roy. He'd watched Roy leave the bar in a jacked-up truck. Unless Roy had borrowed somebody else's car, or had a car of his own, and was waiting outside of JoJo's apartment. What would he hope to gain? Or was it even Roy? The man behind the wheel didn't look nearly as large as the six-feet-seven Roy.

Or was Max getting punchy like JoJo? He drove around the block again, pulled out his cellphone and called JoJo.

She answered on the third ring. "Hello?"

"Hey, JoJo, this is Max." He hesitated, not really wanting to get her stirred up if the lurker was just another apartment complex resident. Then again, it didn't hurt to be overly cautious.

"Did you forget your way to the grocery store?" she asked.

"No, I'm still outside your apartment building. I just wanted to make sure that you're all right." As soon as the words were out of his mouth, he realized how lame they sounded.

She chuckled. "I'm fine like every other night that I come home by myself, but thanks for asking."

"Do me a favor," he said.

"What's that?"

"Without being too obvious, look through your front window. There's a vehicle backed into a space directly across from your apartment. Do you recognize that a vehicle? Is it a regular in the parking lot?"

"Give me a minute," she said. "Okay, I'm at my window. I'm peeking through. Are you talking about the dark one that's backed up against the bushes?"

His grip on the steering wheel tightened. "Yes."

"I'm not sure I've seen that one before, but then again, I don't really know everybody in the apartment complex or their vehicles. It never dawned on me to watch them."

His gut knotted. "Well, just for grins, keep an eye on him and keep me on the line for a little while."

"You really need to go to the grocery store and go home," JoJo said.

"I agree, but I got you this far. I don't want anything to happen to you."

"Thank you for that sentiment. I have a can of mace and a handgun. Just so you know, I'm also licensed to carry."

"Is that handgun loaded?" he asked.

She didn't answer immediately. "Maybe."

"Do me a favor and load it. Have the mace handy, and double check your locks."

She snorted. "And I thought I was a scaredy cat."

"You started my paranoia when you flipped me."

JoJo chuckled. "I told you I was sorry. Or is this payback for landing you flat on your backside?"

"No, not at all," he said, "I just don't trust Roy. He doesn't look like a guy who would take that kind of rejection without retaliating."

"Well, thank you for caring," she said, "but you really should go on. You've done your job by alerting me. I can take it from here."

"Okay, but you have my number. If you need anything, you call me. I'll still be in town for a few minutes more to make that run to the grocery store."

"I'll keep that in mind, and thank you for caring," she said.

"I'll see you in the morning, if I don't see you sooner," he said. "I'm looking forward to our ATV trip."

"Goodnight, Max."

Max ended the call and drove around the block one more time. The guy was still there in the parking lot. Instead of driving past, he pulled in and parked right next to the guy. From what he could see through the darkened windows, the man was not on his cellphone, and it didn't sound like his radio was on. So why he was sitting there staring up at the apartment building?

Max couldn't find a good reason. So, he sat there until the driver next to him cranked up his engine and drove away.

Max's cellphone rang. It was JoJo's number.

"You don't give up, do you?" JoJo said.

Max chuckled. "No, I don't."

"Well, that car's gone now," she said. "I think it's safe to say that you can go to the grocery store."

"You'll let me know if he comes back?" Max asked.

"You'll be the first on my phone tree," she said. "Goodnight, Max."

"Goodnight, JoJo. See ya tomorrow."

He drove to the grocery store, picked up what he needed, and then drove out to the ranch, half-expecting a phone call from JoJo at any moment. When he didn't get one, he sighed. Yeah, he was probably just making it all up in his head.

He'd had gut feelings before, but maybe his gut had it wrong this time. The day he'd fallen from the cliff, his intuition had told him it was a bad day to be out there. He'd ignored it, and he'd paid the price.

Max's gut told him that the man sitting in the car had a nefarious purpose. Was it aimed toward JoJo? Max couldn't be certain. Hopefully, the guy hadn't gone back to the apartment building after Max had left.

JoJo PEEKED around the edge of the blinds and watched as the car Max had identified remained in the parking lot. Even though Max had said he was leaving, he'd come back and parked next to that car.

JoJo smiled. The man didn't give up.

Max's truck sat next to the sedan until that driver

decided he'd had enough and left. If it were anybody else, JoJo might have accused Max of lurking himself. But he left after the other vehicle left.

JoJo's heart swelled.

Once both vehicles had gone, she left her vigil at the window and headed for the shower. In the bathroom, she stripped out of her clothes, turned on the shower faucet to hot and stepped beneath the spray.

JoJo tipped back her head, letting water run down her face over her shoulders and down over her breasts. That heat that she'd felt at her core, earlier with Max, built again. She closed her eyes and imagined his hands, instead of the water, feathering across her skin, over her breasts and down her torso to the juncture of her thighs. How would she react if she lay naked with him? Would she freak out and run? Or would she lie stiff as a board, dreading his touch, afraid of what would come next? Would she ever react normally again to a man's touch? Would she ever crave a man's hands on her body?

Though she felt the urge and the aching need to be touched, she was too afraid to act on it. If she wanted sexual relief, she could pleasure herself, and she proceeded to, letting her hand trail down to that juncture between her thighs to stroke that very special spot over and over again, while thinking about Max and how it would feel to have him do this.

The more she imagined him, the hotter she grew.

She stroked herself, increasing the pressure and pace, getting faster and faster, her body tensing, her breath coming in ragged gasps. Water rushed over her head and eyes, warm rivulets streaming over her naked skin. When she rocketed over the edge, she let out a little cry.

"Max."

JoJo rode the wave all the way to the end. When she could breathe normally again and her pulse slowed, she turned the water to cool, barely chilling the fire that the Green Beret soldier had inspired. Her lips quirked up on the corners. What would he think if he knew that she had come while she was thinking of him? Would he be turned on or would he be appalled? Fortunately, he'd never find out.

She dried off, slipped a T-shirt over her head and pulled on panties and a pair of soft shorts. She wondered what it would feel like to be comfortable in your own skin and feel safe enough to sleep in the nude. With a rapist still on the loose and a strange car having sat in the parking lot, she didn't dare test the theory.

After she brushed her teeth, JoJo walked back to the living room to doublecheck the locks on her door. One last time, she checked through the blinds. Her breath caught. The dark sedan was back in the same spot.

For a long moment, JoJo stared down at the vehicle, willing it to go away. She wished Max would return with his truck, sit next to the car and make the man go away.

She found herself reaching for her cellphone. Max would want her to call him. She hesitated. Hadn't she told him she could handle things on her own? And if she called him, was that handling it on her own?

No.

She couldn't rely on Max. It wasn't his responsibility to take care of her. She needed to learn how to take care of herself, to trust in her own strength and abilities.

JoJo laid the phone on the counter, returned to the front window and peeked through the blinds.

The car was still there.

She studied it for a long time. She couldn't tell whether a driver sat inside or if it was empty. If it was empty, had the person gone into one of the apartments? Or was he lurking, waiting for her to go to bed to break into her apartment?

Her head spun at the thought.

More than likely, she was worrying over nothing. Just in case, she pulled a chair in front of the door. JoJo grabbed her cellphone, went to her bedroom, closed her door and locked it. She moved another chair in front of that door. Standing in the middle of her bedroom, she looked around. What more could she do?

Her eyes narrowed as her gaze landed on her nightstand. She crossed to it, removed her handgun from the top drawer and checked the magazine. Yes, it was full, and it had plenty of bullets in case she missed the first shot. Her can of mace stood on the nightstand as well.

For the next thirty minutes, she paced her bedroom. If she called the cops to report a car in the parking lot, wouldn't she look stupid if that person was actually a resident of the apartment complex? She had no reason to call the sheriff's department unless somebody actually broke into her apartment.

JoJo paced some more, straining her ears to listen for any signs of somebody trying to force their way into her apartment. She couldn't move chairs in front of the windows. Somebody could break the glass and climb through. She'd hear that for sure. She kept her cellphone beside her, her finger ready to hit 911.

After a while, she grew tired of the pacing and laid down in the bed, pulling the blankets up to her chin. Again, she thought about calling Max. Maybe she should call Emily or RJ and talk with them. She might have been better off if Max had never pointed out the vehicle in the parking lot. At least she could be blissfully sleeping by now, unaware of any danger that might be lurking. Instead, she lay in her bed with one hand on her gun, the other one pulling her blanket up to her chin. Eleven o'clock turned into twelve o'clock, twelve o'clock into one, and still she remained staring up at the ceiling.

Sometime after that she must have fallen asleep, because she immediately fell into her nightmare. She lay in the cold dirt. Her body aching, unable to move as somebody shoveled dirt on top of her. The more he shoveled, the heavier the blanket of dirt grew until she could barely breathe. She tried to look at the man, to study his face, to commit it to memory so that she could tell others when she got back to civilization. They needed to know what this man was capable of and keep him from doing it again. Before he covered her head, he leaned close to her and whispered.

"Now, you die."

"No," she tried to say.

She tried again to tell him *no, I'm not going to die. I am going to get out of this, and I'm going to tell everybody that you were the one who did this.* But when she opened her mouth, nothing came out. Nothing but dust.

His face was in the shadows, a gray blob that she couldn't focus on. She had to see him, she had to know who he was. He had to be somebody who was on their military base. Therefore, he had to be one of their own. Then he stepped back, lifted the shovel and tossed more dirt on her face, on her head, over her eyes, until all was dark. With every breath she took, she inhaled dust. She couldn't breathe. She couldn't struggle. She couldn't move.

"This is a dream," JoJo told herself. "Wake up. This is a dream. You survived this once, you'll live again. Wake up, JoJo."

But she couldn't. She was trapped in the darkness, unable to escape.

"Max," she said, if not in words, then in her mind. "I need you."

JoJo woke up the next morning with a headache and the sound of her alarm ringing incessantly. She blinked her eyes open and stared up at the ceiling she'd stared at most of the night. As far as she could tell, nobody had broken into her apartment, and she had just laid awake half the night worrying over nothing.

She tucked her handgun back in the drawer of her nightstand, along with her mace. On second thought, she took out the mace and put it in her purse in the kitchen.

Tired from her sleepless night, JoJo dressed quickly, knowing she needed to get out to the ranch early this morning since they had so much to do. And frankly, she wanted to be back at the ranch with the people who made her feel safe. When she was ready, she made her way to the front door and removed the chair from underneath the handle. Before she unlocked the door, she peeked out the blinds. The car was gone.

She unlocked the door and opened it. Something caught her attention on the door frame. It appeared as if it was splintered, like somebody had been digging at it trying to get past the deadbolt. Her stomach roiled, and she slammed the door shut.

CHAPTER 6

"Max, I'm glad I caught you." Jake was just leaving the breakfast table with his coffee cup headed for the kitchen as Max entered the dining room.

"Mornin', Jake," Max said. "What's up?"

"I'm making a run into the Springs to meet with our new guy, Cage Weaver."

Max smiled. "So, he agreed to come onboard?"

Jake nodded. "Yes, he did."

Max tipped his head to one side. "Aren't you worried that we don't have any work yet for any of us?"

Jake shook his head. "No. Hank wanted me to get people in place, because he's positive we're going to have a very busy schedule before we know it. He's got feelers out to all his contacts. Shouldn't be long."

"Good. I hate taking his money for nothing."

"Trust me, it won't be long before we're busy."

Jake set his mug of coffee on the dining table. "Weaver was eager to get started and asked if he could assist with the event this weekend. Since he's having his vehicle worked on, I'm going to go pick him up and bring him out here."

"Does Gunny have room for him to stay at the lodge with us?" Max asked.

"I'm putting him up at the casino for the weekend nights, but he'll be working here during the day and through the evenings. He'll have my truck to get back and forth."

Max nodded. "That's good. I'm sure Gunny and RJ can use all the help they can get. I'll be out and about today with JoJo. She wanted to make a run through the trails for the ATV tour on Saturday."

Jake gave him a twisted grin. "Tell you what, you meet with the new guy. I'll go out on the trails with JoJo. That sounds like more fun."

"Ha." Max shook his head. "No way. I haven't been up in the mountains since my accident. I'm kind of looking forward to it."

Jake nodded, his smile disappearing. "It'll be good for you."

Max hoped so. He missed the crisp mountain air and the bright blue skies around the peaks.

RJ emerged from the kitchen carrying a plate of fluffy yellow scrambled eggs. "Well, there you are. Just in time. I hope you're hungry."

"You know you don't have to cook my meals for me. I can do that myself," Max said.

RJ shrugged. "It doesn't take any more time to throw a couple more eggs into a pan of scrambled eggs. But if you want to cook my breakfast tomorrow, I won't say no." She winked.

"You're on," he said.

She set the platter of eggs in the middle of the table and turned back to the kitchen. "However, you two can put the cutlery out. I'll be right back out with plates."

"I'll lay out the silverware," Jake offered.

Max hurried to open the swinging door for RJ. "Let me help you with the plates and glasses."

"Deal," she said.

Max followed RJ into the kitchen.

"You're going to need a good breakfast when you go ATV riding with JoJo," RJ said. "You're guaranteed to work up an appetite."

"How so?" Max asked.

"Well, she'll be taking the chainsaw with her in case there are any trees on the path and a shovel to fill in any washes."

Max nodded. "Nice to know. Forewarned is forearmed."

RJ grinned. "That's right, especially with JoJo."

"What time does she usually get in?" Max asked.

RJ pulled plates down from a cabinet. "What do you mean?"

"I mean, what time does she usually show up here?"

"Oh, well, she's already out in the barn."

He frowned. "She comes in that early, and then stays as late as she does at the Watering Hole?"

"Not usually, but since we have this event going on this weekend, she promised to come in early and stay late. She likes being here. I think she likes to tinker on all the machines we have that aren't working. I don't know what we did without her, but then our machinery is getting older, and Gunny has less and less time to work on it. And JoJo is so much faster and better at it. She's amazing with machines. They trained her well in the Army."

"Some people just take a lot of training, and others have a natural knack for it," Max said.

"That would be JoJo."

Max filled glasses with orange juice and carried them out to the dining room. RJ carried the plates, while Jake set the table with cutlery.

Then they were seated and eating the scrambled eggs, bacon and biscuits that RJ had prepared.

"Where's Gunny this morning?" Jake asked.

RJ grinned. "He's out mowing the shoulders of the road to make sure it's nice and groomed for when the guests arrive. He wants the place to make a good first impression."

"What time is the politician arriving?" Max asked.

"Sometime after lunch," RJ said. "Gunny's got a

whole list of stuff he wants to get done before they get here."

"Make sure you let us take some of those tasks off your hands," Jake said.

"Right," Max said. "I'm not sure what time JoJo wants to go out on the ATVs, but if I have time before, I can help out."

"If you could take the dishes after breakfast, I'll get upstairs and make sure the rooms are in order."

"I can do dishes," Max said.

"And I'll be back before noon," Jake said. "Weaver, the new guy, and I will help out with anything after that."

They finished breakfast, and RJ went upstairs.

Jake headed into Colorado Springs to make his appointment with Cage Weaver, the newest member of the Brotherhood Protectors.

Max carried the plates and glasses into the kitchen, quickly washed the dishes and put them away in the cabinets. Once he'd finished, Max headed out to the barn. It took him a moment, but he found JoJo at the back of the barn in one of the stalls. Instead of horses, there were a couple of ATVs parked there.

JoJo had the engine cover off of one and parts strewn all over one corner of the stall. Her hands were greasy, and she had a dark smudge across her cheek. Instead of making JoJo look dirty, it made Max think how cute she was.

With a battery-operated lantern hanging from a hook in the corner, she worked on the engine. All her concentration was focused on what she was doing. She didn't seem to notice him right away, so he used that time to study her. He wasn't sure if it was the shadows thrown by the light or just natural that she had dark circles beneath her eyes, more so than yesterday. Rather than startle her again by touching her shoulder, he cleared his throat to make his presence known.

Her head jerked up, her eyes widening. "Oh," she said, "it's you."

"I came out to see if there was anything I could do to help."

"As a matter of fact, there is," she said, pushing the hair out of her face with her greasy hand, making another smudge across her forehead. Can you hand me that socket wrench kit at your feet?"

He scooped up the plastic tool case and carried it across to her.

She selected several of the sockets and tried them on the bolt she was working on until she found the right one, fitted it to the tool and tightened the bolt. She checked the oil on the machine, primed the pump, and then cranked the starter. After several chugs, the engine roared to life.

"Watch out," she said. "Coming through."

Max stepped to the side as JoJo drove the ATV through the open stall door out into the center of the barnyard. She shifted into neutral, hit the parking brake and left it running. She went back to the other one, started the engine and pulled it out to the center of the barn beside the first, again leaving it running. Both of the four wheelers had metal baskets on the front and back. She walked to the tack room and emerged from it carrying a chainsaw.

JoJo leaned her head toward the barn. "There's a shovel inside. If you could get that and a pickaxe, we can load up. While you're at it, grab a couple bungee cords to tie them down. If you could make sure that everything is battened down, I'm going up to the lodge for a moment."

"I'll take care of it," Max said.

JoJo left him with the two four-wheelers running and jogged up to the lodge.

Max spent the next ten minutes tying things down on the ATVs and just looking around the barn to see what else was left to do. All of the horses were in the pasture and the horse stalls were clean, with fresh wood chips strewn across the floor. Everything had a place, and everything was in its place. Max grinned. He suspected that had a lot to do with Gunny and his Marine background.

JoJo returned carrying a small cooler. She ducked into the tack room and emerged with a bungee cord and tied the cooler to the front of her ATV. "Are you ready?" she asked.

"I am."

She leaned her head toward the other ATV. "That one's yours. I'll get the gate."

He mounted the ATV, briefly studied the controls, released the brake, and gave it some gas, following her out of the barnyard.

She pulled up sideways to the gate, unlocked the latch, pushed it open and drove her ATV through. When she'd cleared the gate on the other side, she dismounted and waited for him to pass through, and then closed the gate behind him.

He waited for her to remount then followed her away from the lodge and barn across a pasture and into the trees. A narrow trail wove between the tree trunks and, eventually, led up a hill. With nothing blocking their paths, they were able to cover quite a bit of distance until they came to a small ghost town.

Jake had mentioned something about the ghost town. He'd been up there with RJ and a group of ranch guests. The town had been built to support mining activities in the area, and there were plenty of trails left over from many years ago when men worked the mines. There was even a mineshaft on the property, in which Jake and RJ had been trapped at one point. Gunny had since been out to make sure that the cover over the entrance was in place and not easily removed. In another stand of trees, JoJo stopped her ATV and dismounted. A large tree branch had fallen over the track. Max climbed off his ATV and unstrapped the chainsaw.

JoJo approached him. "Do you know how to run one of those?"

Max nodded. "I grew up in the country. I did my share of clearing. I know how to run a chainsaw."

"Then, if you'll cut, I'll haul," she said.

And he went to work sawing away at the large branch, breaking it down into pieces that JoJo hauled off the path into the woods. When he was done, he strapped the chainsaw back on the front of the ATV. JoJo had already mounted hers and was pulling away, so he hurried to catch up.

JoJo drove until she reached a wide valley and descended to its bottom where a mountain stream trickled over rocks. She parked her ATV next to the stream and dismounted.

Max did the same. "What needs to be done here?"

She grinned and pulled the cooler off the front of the ATV. "Lunch." They'd been working so hard that he hadn't realized so much time had passed. His stomach rumbled, reminding him that he did need to eat. "I didn't even think about it, but I'm glad you brought something."

She grimaced. "I'm not much of a cook, but I did make wraps with some lettuce and tomatoes in them. Just enough to get us by until we can get back to the lodge."

"Sounds good. And I'm not at all picky." He gave her a crooked grin. "I used to like chow hall food."

She smiled. "So did I. Anything I didn't have to

cook. Although, some chow halls were better than others."

"For the most part, they served some decent food," Max said. "But that's just me."

"And me." JoJo nodded and fished a foil covered wrap out of the cooler and tossed it to him. He missed the catch and had to bend to pick the wrap off the ground. He winced when he came back up.

"Sorry," JoJo said.

He grimaced. "It's not your fault."

"Let me do it right this time." She brought him another deli wrap and handed it to him rather than threw it at him. She pulled one more out of the cooler for herself, unwrapped it and sank her teeth into it. They ate in silence, sitting on a rock ledge next to the stream, listening to the gentle sound of the bubbling brook. JoJo's face had softened, and she actually looked happy for the first time since Max had met her.

"You like this place, don't you?" he asked.

She nodded. "It makes me feel… peaceful."

"I can see that," he said. "It does have that sense. There are a lot of things in this world that make us feel less than peaceful."

Her lips twisted. "Like cars sitting out in the apartment parking lot? And trucks pulling in next to them until they leave?"

He shook his head. "You saw that, huh?"

She nodded. "I did and thank you."

He shrugged. "I would've done it for anyone."

"Yeah." JoJo glanced down at her food and lowered her voice. "I almost called you when he came back."

Max shot a glance toward her. "He came back?"

"Yes, he did. I took a shower, and by the time I got out, he was back in the parking lot, backed into the space where he could stare at my apartment. Not that I know that's what he was doing, but it sure seemed kind of creepy to me."

"JoJo, you should have called me," Max said.

She laughed. "I thought about calling the sheriff's department, but what would I have told them? For all I know, somebody who lived in the apartment building was sitting in that car or had parked that car and had gone up to their apartment. I would've looked a fool, and if I'd called you, I would've gotten you worked up over nothing."

"JoJo..."

"It's okay. Better safe than sorry. I moved a chair in front of the door, and I slept with my gun next to me."

He shook his head. "You really should have called me. I would've come back."

"I told you..."

Max raised his hands. "You can handle it. You can take care of yourself. But everybody needs a friend, and I'm telling you I can be that friend for you. For the record, I'm not asking for strings or anything else. I'm just worried about you. I left and I didn't want to."

"Why?" she asked.

He shook his head. "No, you'd get mad if I said anything."

"I'll get madder if you don't," she said.

"I don't know. I just felt like you were vulnerable, even though I know you can kick my ass. Not only does everybody need a friend, but they also need someone who'll watch their six."

She chewed on the last bite of her wrap and swallowed. "Well, I appreciate the sentiment. What was kind of scary about the whole thing was when I got up this morning and opened my front door it appeared that somebody had been scraping at the lock with something sharp."

Max swore. "Dammit, JoJo, you should've called me."

"I didn't know he was going to try and break in that way, and I didn't hear anything. Plus, I had the bedroom door locked, and again, I had my gun next to me. If he had managed to get the door open, he would've knocked the chair over. I'd have heard it when it crashed to the ground. Then I would've had my gun out and put a couple of holes in him."

"Wow, JoJo," Max said, "I don't like the sound of that."

She grinned. "What? The part about putting a couple holes in him?"

He shook his head. "No, the part about somebody breaking into your apartment while you're in it. You should speak with Gunny and RJ and ask them if you can stay the next few nights here at the ranch."

JoJo pressed her lips into a thin line. "I already did. I'm staying."

"Good. Otherwise, I would have to camp out in your apartment parking lot."

Her brow furrowed. "You'd do that?"

Max nodded. "I would."

"Again," she said, "why?"

"I don't know. I think you're pretty special and sassy, and I'd hate to see you get hurt."

She wadded up her foil wrapper, rose to her feet and put it into the cooler. She retrieved a small bottle of water and started to toss it to him, then rethought it and handed it to him instead and got another one out for herself.

JoJo shrugged. "It works out for the best anyway, for me to stay at the lodge with everybody coming in this weekend."

Max nodded, glad that she was going to stay. That way he wouldn't have to park out in that parking lot, and he could keep an eye on her while she was at the ranch. "Do you think it was Roy trying to get into your apartment?"

"I can't think of any other suspect. I don't know if I've pissed off anybody else." JoJo pinched the bridge of her nose. "That's why I try to be nice to the bar patrons, even when they're jerks."

"Well, I'll work in the bar with you tonight and keep an eye out to see if there's anyone there who acts suspicious."

She dropped her hand to her side. "You don't have to do that."

"I know I don't, Max said. "But I'm your friend, and I've got your six. How much farther will we be traveling on this trail with the guests?"

She stared up a hillside. "Probably up to the old mine, and then we'll turn around and come back. I think that's far enough to take the others. Although, there is a really pretty bluff area that I'd like to take them to so that they can see the view from there."

"You lead, I'll follow," he said.

She climbed aboard her four-wheeler and took off.

He did the same, following her. They made it up to the old mine where she made a circle in front of it. Without stopping, she pushed on, climbing higher up the mountain.

When they reached the top of a ridge where the ground leveled off, she got down off her ATV and walked toward the edge of a cliff.

Max killed his engine, jumped off and hurried after her. He hadn't been near the edge of a cliff since he'd fallen. Seeing JoJo so close to the drop-off made his heart pound. It shouldn't have. How many times had he stood at the edge of a cliff, looking down, judging the route he would take and where he would anchor his ropes to descend? He caught up with her before she got to the edge. He started to reach out for her and remembered how she'd reacted before.

"JoJo," he said.

She turned to face him. "Yes?"

He thought how ridiculous he'd sound by saying don't get too close to the brink, but he'd rather do that than have her fall over. "Be careful," he said instead.

"Always am," she said. "It's an over three-hundred-foot drop to the bottom of the gorge here." Her brow furrowed. "Does it bother you to get close to the edges of cliffs since your fall?"

He sighed. "I haven't rappelled since then, nor have I climbed any mountains. For me, personally, I'd probably be okay standing by the edge of the cliff."

She smiled. "But it bothers you that I'm standing so close, doesn't it?"

He nodded. "In the past, I was eager to try my hand at cliffs like this and to teach the young soldiers how to navigate them. Both up and down."

"And now?" JoJo asked.

He shrugged. "I really don't know. I haven't tried." He touched a hand to his leg. "I don't know how this will hold up."

"You obviously liked mountaineering, or you wouldn't have done it for so long."

He smiled. "Believe it or not, I have a fear of heights."

Her eyes widened. "Seriously? Isn't it kind of hard to be someone who climbs mountains and still have a fear of heights?"

He nodded. "It forced me to confront my fears. I always felt stronger afterward. I beat my fears when I met the challenge."

JoJo's brow furrowed. "So, confronting your fears helps make you stronger?"

"It did in my case," he said, "but then I got cocky."

"Is that what happened?"

"I got complacent about checking my gear. I assumed it was all in good working order. When you're stepping over the ledge, it's not a good time to discover a key piece of equipment isn't in good working order. Not when you're two-hundred and fifty feet above the bottom of a cliff." He stared out across the mountains. Blue filled the sky, in stark contrast to the ragged peaks. It was hard to have bad thoughts when you were surrounded by so much beauty.

"Will you ever climb mountains again?" JoJo asked.

"Probably, if my body cooperates."

"Will your leg ever fully recover?"

"Probably not," he said. "The doc thinks I'll always have a limp. And it will take a lot of effort to build back my strength. But I'm working on it."

She tilted her head, her gaze meeting his. "And then you'll confront your fear again?"

He nodded. "I will. Have you ever thought about challenging your fears?"

It was as if the light in her eyes shut off. She turned away. "I think it would be easier to climb a mountain." In other words, she didn't want to talk about it. "We should be getting back. Our guests should be arriving soon. We might want to be there when they do."

And just like that, she shut him down. And it was fair. He had no right to butt into her life and figure out her problems for her. If anything, he should know you can only resolve your own problems.

They mounted the ATVs and started down the mountain, heading back to the lodge. The haunted look in JoJo's eyes stayed with Max for the rest of the day. He'd really like to know what had happened to her. It might help him understand why she acted the way she did, and then, maybe, he could help her in some small way. Obviously, she wasn't ready to talk about it. He hoped that she would want to talk about it someday with him. He knew she was hurting over something, and he wanted to take her pain away. Why? He didn't know. She was practically a stranger to him, but he understood pain.

CHAPTER 7

Confront your fears?

Ha! JoJo thought. How does one confront your fears when you were raped? You don't challenge that kind of fear unless you can stand face to face with the one who did it. That would be the only way to confront that kind of fear. Until then, every man she met could be her attacker.

JoJo barely saw the scenery as she drove back down the trail all the way to the barn. Her thoughts leaped back and forth between Max's issues with his accident and his subsequent hesitancy to get back into mountaineering, and then her own issues with her attack and her resistance to getting back into life.

Or attempting any type of relationship.

She could tell that Max wanted to help her. But what had happened to her was a lot more personal than falling off a mountain.

When she arrived at the barn, several other vehicles were parked outside near the house. She recognized the one belonging to Jake. Beside it was a truck. Jake and another man stood in front of that one. A dark SUV was parked beside the truck with a big campaign sign on the door proclaiming Lawrence Stover's candidacy for the US Senate, encouraging whoever read the sign to vote for him.

Max pulled up behind her, killed the engine, climbed off his ATV and walked over to the two men standing by the truck. He shook hands with Jake and the new guy.

JoJo opened the barn door and parked her ATV in the last stall on the left. She removed her helmet and laid it on the seat. Then she bent over and ran her fingers through her hair, lifting it off her scalp where the helmet had pressed it close. Not that she was trying to look good for anyone in particular, she told herself. It wasn't as if she were trying to impress Max, Jake or the new Brotherhood Protector.

She exited the barn and headed toward Max's ATV.

Max waved and said, "I'll take care of that in a minute. Come meet Weaver."

JoJo would rather have stuck with the machines, but he'd put her on the spot, so she walked across to be introduced.

"Weaver, this is Ms. Ramirez," Jake said. "She works for Gunny. JoJo, this is Cage Weaver. He just came on board with the Brotherhood Protectors here in Colorado. He also agreed to help out this weekend. Anywhere you can think of that he can help, let us know. Or let RJ or Gunny know he's available."

She searched the man's face, looking for any sign of recognition in her own eyes. Nothing in the shape of his face or his eyes triggered any memories, but then again whoever attacked her could be anybody as long as she couldn't remember his face. "Prior military?" she asked.

"Yes, ma'am," he said.

"Branch?"

"Army."

Nothing in his face, Jake's, or Max's triggered any kind of memories. She didn't expect it with Jake, him being a SEAL. However, SEALs could have been temporarily located where she'd been deployed.

From what Jake had said about Max, he'd been stationed here in Colorado around the time of JoJo's attack. He had been training younger soldiers in the art of mountain warfare. The possibility of Max being in the same place that JoJo had deployed was pretty slim. But she didn't know anything about Weaver, and him being Army...he could've been deployed where she was. She'd have to find out more. Still, she hesitated to take his hand in a firm handshake, but she ultimately did.

His grip was firm and blessedly short, and he released her hand. "Nice to meet you, Ms. Ramirez."

"Please, people call me JoJo."

He nodded. "JoJo."

Jake glanced up at the house and tipped his head toward the two gentlemen walking down to the barn with Gunny. "That must be Stover and his campaign manager."

Jake, Max, Weaver and JoJo met them halfway.

Gunny turned to the man at his side. "Mr. Stover, these are some of the people who will be helping out this weekend. Ms. Ramirez works for us here at the ranch. She's quite a good mechanic, and she helps out in the bar at night. She'll also be with my daughter RJ on the ATV tour Saturday."

Stover smiled and held out his hand. "Ms. Ramirez, nice to meet you."

JoJo placed her hand in his. Almost immediately, she wanted to jerk it back, but she forced herself to hold on and shake the politician's hand.

His palm was cool and dry, as if he'd just stepped out of an air-conditioned SUV. "Gunny tells me that most of the people helping out this weekend are prior military. Does that include you, Ms. Ramirez?"

She nodded.

"Which branch?" he asked.

"Army." JoJo pulled her hand free of his.

His smile broadened. "I, too, was Army. Recently retired. We'll have to visit for a while and figure out where we might have been stationed together. Who knows, we may have worked together."

"Unless you were in the motor pool, I doubt it," she said.

He turned back to his aide. "Ms. Ramirez, this is my aide, Miles Curry. He'll be able to answer most questions anyone might need to direct to me, if I'm not available."

Mr. Curry shook her hand, his eyes narrowing. "Nice to meet you, Ms. Ramirez."

His face wasn't familiar, but something about his voice...

That was the trouble with losing her memory. She tried to read too much into everything. Every prior military man was a suspect. She just didn't know which one was the actual bastard who'd attempted to murder her.

The politician and his aide turned to the three men. Gunny introduced them. "These guys are with a start-up that just leased my basement. You might be able to use their services. They're the Brotherhood Protectors Colorado Division. From what I understand, they'll provide security services. But here, talk to Jake. He's the one in charge, and he'll be better able to explain what exactly they can do for you."

JoJo hung around for a few seconds more, hoping to be able to hear more of the aide's voice, but Stover was doing all the talking, and they listened as Jake talked about the Brotherhood Protectors and what their role was and how they could help politicians and others with their security needs by providing bodyguards or security personnel.

As the men talked, JoJo studied the politician and his aide. She didn't know any other politicians, but this one's military background was apparent. He stood straight with his shoulders back and his head held high, as did his aide. She wondered if he was also prior service and, if so, what branch of the military?

After a few minutes she excused herself. "I think I'll go help RJ clean up the bar and get it ready for tonight's crowd." She turned to Gunny. "Everything's ready as far as machinery goes. All the ATVs are running, and I can hook up the trailer to the tractor tomorrow morning for the hayride."

He nodded. "Thank you, JoJo."

JoJo escaped with a creepy feeling crawling over her skin. Nothing about the new Brotherhood Protector triggered any weird feeling, but the politician and his aide…

JoJo's stomach clenched. Something about them didn't ring true. But was it because they were politicians, and JoJo had a natural distrust of anyone who was a politician? They tended to be so focused on getting elected, they never seemed to show their true selves. At least, that's how she saw it. Most of them seemed to go around kissing babies when they really didn't like children at all.

No matter how she felt about Stover and his aide,

she had to keep a game face on through the weekend while helping Gunny and RJ make this event a success. If Stover got elected, he'd have connections, and he could recommend the Lost Valley Ranch to his friends. That would bring in more business for RJ and Gunny. JoJo would keep her opinions and her weird feelings to herself.

She entered the Watering Hole through the back door and found RJ in the kitchen scrubbing the stove after what appeared to have been a busy lunch.

"Need some help?" JoJo asked.

RJ looked up, sweat pebbling her brow. "You bet I do. Grab a scrub pad and help me with the pans in the sink. The weekend guests ended up arriving right at the end of the lunch rush. I told Gunny go on, I'd take care of the cleanup. Did you get to meet them?"

JoJo nodded. "I did."

"What did you think?" RJ asked.

"I think we'll have a busy weekend," she said.

RJ shook her head. "That's not what I meant. Is he the kind of guy you would vote for?"

Her stomach clenched again. "I don't know anything about him, what he stands for or what his platform is."

RJ nodded. "I guess we might figure that out over this weekend."

JoJo pulled up her sleeves, tied an apron on over her clothes and went to work scrubbing the pans in the sink.

"Emily called and asked how she could help this weekend," RJ said.

JoJo's brow furrowed

"I'm looking forward to seeing her," RJ smiled. "It's been a while since she's been out to the ranch. You know she lived here while you were on active duty, right?"

JoJo nodded. "Gunny had said something to that effect."

"Are you two doing all right together?" RJ asked. "Not that your interaction with Emily is any of my business."

JoJo nodded. "We are getting along fine."

"I don't know what kind of therapist she is, but she's a good friend. She really cares about people, and she's a good listener." RJ chuckled. "I guess that's a good thing since she's in the business she's in."

JoJo nodded.

"The offer is still open." RJ glanced over at JoJo. "Anytime you need a friend to talk to, I'm here for you."

JoJo glanced up from the pan she was scrubbing and smiled. "I know that, and I value your friendship."

"I know deep down you're hurting about something," RJ rushed on. "I wish I could help you with it."

JoJo tensed. "I know that too. And you know I'd do anything for you and Gunny. You're *mi familia.*"

RJ grinned. "I'd give you a big hug right now, but I'm up to my elbows in grease."

JoJo laughed. "Well, thank you. I'd appreciate you not hugging me right now. These clothes have to last the rest of the evening."

"Fine, I'll save it for later," RJ said. "I have a room set aside for you to stay in tonight. And when Emily gets here, I've got a place I can put her up as well. She's going to stay the weekend. If Stover's campaign team is all male, it might get man-heavy. Might be nice to have a few other women around."

"Agreed," JoJo rinsed the pan she'd scrubbed, dried it and put it away. She started on the next one.

RJ sprayed the grill with water and scrubbed some more. "Look, JoJo, I know something happened to you on your last deployment. Something that put you in the hospital. It really would help if I knew what it was so that I can help you to recover from it. I mean, were you injured? Were you taken captive? I just wish I knew," RJ said. "And I wish you felt comfortable enough to tell me. I don't feel much like a friend if I can't help you."

JoJo sighed. What was it Max had said? He'd rappelled and climbed mountains to face his fear of heights. He'd confronted those fears. Maybe it was time that JoJo confronted hers. One of those fears being acceptance. Would people accept her, knowing that she'd been raped? RJ was her dearest and closest friend. If she couldn't accept her, damaged as she was, who could?

JoJo turned to RJ. "I'll tell you, but I'd appreciate if you didn't tell Gunny right now."

"Let me get ready." RJ finished scrubbing, rinsed and dried the grill. Then she washed her hands.

JoJo rinsed the suds off her hands, dried them on a towel and then she stood in front of RJ, trying to find the words to tell her friend what had happened to her.

"First of all," she said, "I'm not exactly sure what happened to me. All I know is what the medic told the nurses and what the nurses told me. This is what I know." She drew in a deep breath and launched into her nightmare. "I was walking out of a shower unit on our base, and the next thing I know I woke up with my face covered in dirt. The medic said that somebody had beaten me, raped me and buried me alive."

CHAPTER 8

RJ's face blanched white. "Dear, sweet Jesus," she said, and she pulled JoJo into her arms. "Why didn't you tell us?"

Like Max feared heights, JoJo had feared rejection. "Though I don't remember the incident, it made me feel dirty," JoJo said, "less human."

RJ hugged her tighter, and then set her at arm's length. "Did they catch the guy who did it?"

JoJo shook her head. "And that's the problem, I can't get closure, knowing he's still out there and capable of doing this to some other female."

"Or coming back to finish you off?" RJ shook her head. "Oh, JoJo."

JoJo's fists tightened. "That thought has occurred to me. He expected me to die."

"And you didn't," RJ said.

"I never went back to my unit. They took me

straight from where they found me to a medical staging unit at an airbase and shipped me out to Ramstein. The only thing I remembered was that my name was JoJo. I didn't recall anything else until I had been in the hospital for a couple of days."

"Oh, JoJo," RJ said, "I wish I had known. I'd have flown to Europe to be with you."

"It took several weeks for most of my memories to come back, but there is one memory that hasn't come back at all, and from what I understand may never come back."

RJ shook her head. "Memories of the incident?"

JoJo nodded. "They say it's the mind and body's way of protecting me. But it doesn't keep me from having nightmares. Until the guy's caught, there will be no closure."

"Why did you take an apartment in town?" RJ asked.

"The nightmares," she said, her tone flat, emotionless. "Sometimes, I wake up screaming."

Tears filled RJ's eyes. "You're staying here," she said. "You're not going back to that apartment. You're staying here with your family. Gunny and I will take care of you."

JoJo shook her head. "I don't want that. I need to know that I can live on my own. That I can take care of myself."

"That's why you took the Krav Maga lessons?"

JoJo nodded. "Absolutely. I was afraid to go

anywhere, to even step outside of my apartment. I don't feel safe anywhere."

"Not even here on the ranch?" RJ asked.

"It's the closest I feel to safe, but there are so many people who come through here, I can't feel comfortable all the time."

RJ muttered a curse. "It doesn't help when a jerk like Roy is pulling you onto his lap at the Watering Hole. You and I should switch places. You can man the bar, and I'll wait on the tables."

"No," JoJo said. "I don't want your pity, and I don't need you to treat me like fine china. I need to relearn how to live in this world, how to trust that I can take care of myself."

"Did your unit launch an investigation?" RJ asked.

"Once I figured out who I was and what unit I belonged to, they did. They launched an investigation, and it's come up with nothing so far."

RJ crossed her arms over her chest, her brow furrowing. "You have no memory at all of the man who attacked you?"

JoJo shook her head.

"Well, I'm glad that you've had Emily to talk to in the meantime," RJ said. "If anyone can help you, she can. She's got a heart of gold, and she's really good at her job from what I hear."

"She wants to try hypnosis," JoJo said. Her stomach roiled at that thought. She wanted to know who'd attacked her, more than anything. And when she remembered?

"How do you feel about that?" RJ asked.

JoJo shrugged. "I don't know. Kind of feel like it's hocus pocus. Does it really work?"

"Does it hurt if it doesn't work? I mean, aren't you willing to try anything to shake those memories loose?"

"That's kind of how I feel," JoJo said. "So, I'm game."

"I'm glad you told me what happened. It helps me to understand the way you reacted when I set you up on that date with Max. I'm sorry I forced you to go to the Sadie Hawkins Dance with him."

"No worries. Actually, Max was very nice. *Is* very nice."

"He seemed to be a gentleman. You took him out on the trails today, didn't you? How'd that go?"

"Good. It was quiet. Just the two of us and the mountains."

"You weren't uncomfortable being alone with him all that time?" RJ asked.

"Not at all." Except for when he'd asked her about why she acted the way she did.

"Once again, I'm sorry I pushed you and Max together."

"And once again, I have to say don't worry about it. I have to confront my fears." JoJo smiled. "And I'm doing okay."

"I'm glad to hear that, and it makes me even madder to think about what Roy did to you and how that must have impacted you."

JoJo touched RJ's arm. "This is one of the reasons why I didn't want to tell you. I don't want you worrying about me. You have enough on your plate."

"How can I not worry about a friend who is more like a sister to me?" RJ asked. "If the situation were reversed, you would feel the same way. And you'd want to find the bastard who'd done that to me. Just like I want to find the bastard who did what he did to you." RJ's eyes narrowed. "You know the Brotherhood Protectors have a computer guru up in Montana. Jake says that he's been able to access records that...well...might not be totally legal to access, like hacking into a system. Maybe he could do some poking around and see what's going on with the investigation."

JoJo shook her head. "I really didn't want anybody else to know about this other than me and the investigators who are handling it." She gave RJ a weak smile. "I didn't even want you to know."

RJ hugged her. "I understand. I still think it's horseshit, but I understand."

JoJo chuckled. Trust RJ to give her honest opinion. "Please, don't be mad at me for not telling you upfront."

"I'm not, but I'm kind of mad at myself for not pushing a little harder to find out sooner. I could've saved you some heartache of going to the Sadie Hawkins Day dance with Max. And you could've been mixing drinks behind the bar, instead of waiting on tables."

"I don't want you to treat me differently just because of what happened."

"Trust me, I won't love you any less. In fact, I'll probably love you even more. You're the sister I never had. I love you, JoJo. I'm so very glad you lived to come back to Colorado. I've missed you so much."

JoJo clapped her hands together. "Okay, enough talk about me. Let's get this place cleaned up. We've got other things to do."

"Yes, ma'am," RJ said and popped a salute. "But you are staying here tonight, aren't you?"

JoJo frowned. "You know, I don't think it's going to get as busy as all that tonight, so I might go on back to my apartment and bring some clothes out with me tomorrow."

"I really think you need to consider staying here tonight. I'll make hot cocoa. We can sit up like we did when we were teenagers and talk about our favorite musical bands and boys."

Oh, to be that teenager again. JoJo wished she could go back and relive it. Maybe she could avoid what had happened to her.

No. She was who she was now based on all her experience in the Army. Good and bad. There was no going back. The only path available was to move forward. "Hold that thought for tomorrow night. Emily will be here too, and we can include her."

RJ grinned. "I'm glad you feel that way. We think a lot of Emily. She, too, is like family to us."

When they'd finished cleaning the kitchen they closed up and walked back to the lodge together.

"You met Stover and his aide as well," JoJo said. "What did you think about them?"

RJ shrugged. "I don't know. He seemed like the typical politician. All smiles and handshakes. He did serve in the military, but he seemed to have made the transition to politician rather quickly." RJ glanced down at her hand. "I didn't like the way he shook my hand."

JoJo laughed. "And how was that?"

"Can't put my finger on it. I just didn't like the way he shook my hand." She looked across at JoJo. "You felt it, too?"

JoJo nodded.

RJ's lips twisted into a wry grin. "We'll just have to leave the hand shaking to the rest of his constituents and make it through the weekend."

JoJo's thoughts exactly.

"We have a couple of hours before we have to man the bar again this evening. What are your plans?" RJ asked.

"I thought I'd tinker in the barn and see if I can get that old rototiller to work."

RJ laughed. "You mean there's a machine out

there you haven't completely overhauled and got running? No, wait. Is it that rototiller that's like fifty thousand years old?"

JoJo smiled. "Yeah, some of the older models are easier to work on."

"Well, don't be a stranger. And if you want anything, let me know. I can bring some lemonade or iced tea out to you."

"I'm good for now but thank you." She just wanted to be alone with her thoughts.

RJ stopped before they were to split off to the lodge and barn. She faced JoJo. "Thank you for letting me in. At least, now, I know what I'm up against, and that's whatever you're up against."

"RJ, this is *my* battle. I have to work through it on my own."

"Sweetie, you're my family. You don't have to do anything alone. I'm here for you." She hugged JoJo and swiped a tear from the corner of her eye. "Say the word, and I'll have Jake contact his guys up in Montana and see if they can do some computer hacking until they find out what's going on with the investigation."

"I'll think about it," JoJo said.

After one last hug, RJ left her and entered the lodge.

JoJo turned and walked down to the barn.

The barn was blessedly empty. In the morning, she'd help RJ bring some of the horses in, help brush them and clean their hooves, so they'd be ready for guests to ride if they should choose. For now, it was just JoJo and the few pieces of machinery that were kept in the barn.

She carried the tool bag over to the old rototiller and systematically disassembled the engine, laying the parts out neatly on a horse blanket beside her. She had just located the faulty part when she heard footsteps behind her. She glanced over her shoulders, half expecting to see Max standing there. Instead, she found Lawrence Stover.

JoJo leapt to her feet and stood with her back to the wall. "Can I help you find something, sir?" she asked, hating that her voice shook. She couldn't be afraid of every man she came into contact with.

"No, thank you. I don't need anything. I just thought I'd poke around and see what was available out here for when my campaign team arrives."

"Well, I'll just leave you to it then," JoJo said. She started to walk around him.

He stuck out his hand and grabbed her arm.

JoJo jerked free.

"Sorry, I didn't mean to startle you," he said. "I just wanted to talk to you for a few minutes."

"If you have questions about the running of the lodge and the ranch, you need to take those to Gunny and RJ. I'm just the hired help."

"My questions aren't about the ranch. I was curious about your service in the military. Seems like we have that in common. So, you worked in the motor pool?" he asked.

She nodded and backed away a few steps rubbing her arm where he'd touched her. "Yes, sir."

"No need for the formality of *yes sir*. We're not on active duty anymore." He smiled. "You can call me Lawrence. How many years were you in?"

"Ten and some change."

"And you got out?" His eyebrows rose. "You were halfway to retirement. Why did you get out?"

She lifted her chin. "I had my reasons."

"Did you deploy?"

She nodded. "Several times. Seems like they need vehicles to work when they're out in the desert."

"That's true. I'm surprised they didn't offer you a big bonus to stay on. It takes a lot to get a mechanic trained up."

They had. Because of her injuries, they'd given her the choice to go back to her unit or to get out before her enlistment date was up. She hadn't wanted to go back to her unit. Not when her attacker hadn't been caught, and it hadn't looked like it would happen anytime soon. She'd chosen to get out and go home.

"When was your last deployment?" he asked.

"Right before I got out of the military." JoJo rubbed her arm. "Why are you asking so many questions?"

"No reason, other than I like to understand the

people I'll hopefully represent. Colorado Springs is filled with military and has quite a strong population of veterans as well. I like to understand them and know what their concerns are. So, Ms. Ramirez, what are your concerns," he asked, "as a veteran?"

She shrugged. "I'd like to see the veterans get the medical care they need, for both their physical and mental health."

He nodded. "That's part of my platform. What else?"

Her eyes narrowed. "I'd like to see them do more to curb and eliminate sexual assault and harassment within the active-duty forces. It's out of control."

The politician's eyes narrowed. "You say that like you've experienced it?"

"I don't know too many females who haven't." She lifted her chin. "Now, if you're finished questioning me, I have work to do." Once again, she tried to walk around him.

He put his hand out to stop her. Rage shot through her system, and she was one second away from throwing the man to the ground when she heard someone call out.

"Hey, JoJo, are you in there?"

Stover dropped his hand from her arm.

JoJo looked over his shoulder to see Max standing in the doorway. "I'm over here," she said.

"Gunny sent me to tell you that he's ready to open the bar. He could use your help since RJ's busy."

"Coming," JoJo said. "Perhaps you can show Mr. Stover around. He seems to want to get to know the place." This time when she stepped around him, he did not put his hand out to stop her.

JoJo hurried out of the barn, throwing a grateful glance toward Max as she left. She'd have to remember to thank him later. Had he not come in when he did, she would've ruined Gunny's and RJ's chances with the politician and any future business he might generate.

MAX WATCHED as JoJo crossed the yard heading toward the Watering Hole before he turned to address Stover. "Is there something in particular you would like to look at?"

The man glanced around the barn. "Not really. I just wanted to see what facilities were available."

"I thought Gunny brought you down to the barn earlier and explained what your team could expect."

"He did, but I wanted to check it out by myself. Take a little more time." He glanced at his watch. "But I guess I need to be back up at the lodge. I'm expecting a phone call."

"Well, if you have any specific questions about how the lodge or ranch are run, you probably need to address those with RJ or Gunny."

Stover cocked an eyebrow. "You mean not Ms. Ramirez?"

"Yes, sir. Gunny and RJ have been here a lot longer. They know all the ins and outs of the ranch and bar operations."

The politician's mouth quirked up on one side. "Do I detect a little protectiveness toward Ms. Ramirez?"

"Ms. Ramirez can take care of herself." But Max would be there to help, if she needed it.

"I mean the woman no harm, if that's what you're insinuating."

Max squared his shoulders. "I'm not insinuating anything. Just stating the facts."

"I'll be sure to direct my questions to RJ and Gunny in the future," Stover said. "Now, if you'll excuse me, I do have that telephone call to catch." The political candidate stepped around Max and headed up to the lodge.

Max hurried to the Watering Hole to check on JoJo.

Instead of waiting tables, she was busy behind the bar mixing drinks for the few patrons who were starting to file into the building. If he had not been mistaken, she'd given him a relieved look when she'd left the barn, which made him wonder what Stover had been up to make JoJo feel nervous. He took a seat at the bar since the rest of the room wasn't that busy and RJ was waiting tables.

"What can I get you?" JoJo asked.

"Nothing I can't get myself." He started to get up.

JoJo held up a hand. "Don't get up. I'll get whatever you want. What is it?"

He sank back onto the barstool. "A cup of coffee would be nice."

She nodded and turned to the pot that was brewing. "It'll be a few minutes before it's done."

"I'm in no hurry," he said. "Was Stover bothering you in the barn?"

Her lips pressed into a thin line. "He asked a lot of questions."

"About what?"

"My military background and what I wanted him to do in reference to veterans."

"And that made you feel nervous?"

She shrugged. "You know me. I don't like to be cornered in any building."

Max chuckled. "I know. I guess the politician didn't get the hint. Why didn't you toss him over your shoulder like you did me?"

"I save my moves to impress the men I like." She set a coffee mug in front of him, turned to retrieve the pot and poured a cup full.

The warm aroma filled the air.

He grinned. "So, that must mean you like me after all."

"At least you learn quickly." Her lips pressed into a thin line. "Some men never learn."

He caught her gaze and held it. "I'd never hurt you, intentionally," he said.

JoJo held his gaze for a long moment, before sighing. "I have to believe you. You've always treated me with care and consideration."

"Except when I stepped on your toes at the dance." He studied her face, not liking the shadows in her eyes. "You know I'll be here tonight in the bar if you need anything."

"Thanks, but I—"

He held up his hand. "I know, you can take care of yourself. But if, for some reason out of your control, you find yourself in trouble, I've got your six."

JoJo drew in a deep breath and let it out. "*Gracias.*" And she meant it. Perhaps she wasn't an island. Having a man like Max as her backup gave her a better chance of surviving.

CHAPTER 9

JAKE AND CAGE Weaver entered the bar and sat at the counter with Max.

"Want to get a table?" Jake asked.

Max didn't really want to. He wanted to stay at the bar and talk with JoJo. Then he reconsidered. She probably needed to be left alone to get her job done.

As the men stood, RJ came by. "There's a table in the corner if you guys would like to move."

"Sounds perfect," Jake said.

Max sat with his back to the wall, facing the bar and JoJo. Every once in a while, she looked up and their gazes met. He hoped that she didn't find him annoying. He smiled reassuringly.

Max focused his attention on the new guy. "So, Weaver, what's your background?"

"Army Ranger," Weaver said.

Max lips twisted. "All right, I won't hold that against you."

Weaver grinned. "And you?"

"Army Green Beret."

Weaver sat back, his arms crossed over his chest. "So, what does that mean? While we do the hard stuff of going in and ferreting out the enemy, you Green Berets teach the natives how to do it themselves."

Max nodded. "That's part of our job. And you left the glamour of being an Army Ranger, why?"

The Ranger's face darkened. "I have my reasons."

"Your choice or Uncle Sam's?" Max asked.

"My choice," Weaver said.

"It's nice to have choices," Max said.

"What about you?" Weaver asked.

"Uncle Sam's choice." Max's jaw tightened. "Medical board."

Weaver shook his head. "That sucks."

"Tell me about it." Max lifted his chin toward Jake. "I'd still be unemployed if Jake hadn't come along and brought me on board with the Brotherhood Protectors."

Weaver laughed. "When Jake came along, I was trying to decide between insurance salesman and convenience store clerk. Both choices sucked. Don't get me wrong. They're both honorable professions."

"But not what you trained for," Max finished.

Weaver nodded. "Not nearly." He turned to Jake, "Although, the jury is still out. I haven't figured out what Brotherhood Protectors are since we haven't gotten our first assignments yet."

Max cast a glance toward the regional leader of the Brotherhood Protectors. "Jake and I got a little taste of it when Gunny's daughter got a little sideways with their neighbor wanting to control the mines in the area."

"Is that right?" Weaver turned his attention to Jake.

Jake nodded. "Protecting RJ became a fulltime job for a short while there."

"And that's what we'll be doing?" Weaver frowned. "Glorified bodyguards?"

Jake grinned. "It's an honorable profession," he said, his lips quirking. "And it's not as easy as you'd think. Like combat, lives are on the line. Only in the civilian world, you're not usually as well armed as we were in the military. You won't always know who the enemy is until you end up trapped in a mine with the entrance caved in by an explosion of dynamite."

Weaver leaned forward. "Seriously?"

Jake nodded.

The new guy sat back in his seat. "Okay then, maybe it won't be as boring as I was thinking. From everything Hank's told me, they've had some pretty interesting assignments up in Montana, and they anticipate having similar work here in Colorado."

"I'm ready to get started," Max said.

"Hank's working on that, and he's spreading the

word. His mega movie star wife rubs elbows with a lot of the rich and famous in Hollywood."

"Then why didn't we set up shop in LA?" Weaver asked.

"There are plenty of security agencies already in LA," Jake said. "With so many rich folks coming out to Colorado and buying up property, they're going to need security agencies like us to protect them and their assets. In the meantime, we have a weekend ahead of us helping out Gunny and RJ with Stover's campaign committee."

"It's outdoors and better than selling insurance," Weaver said. "Hell, almost anything is better than selling insurance."

"Deployments?" Max asked.

"Seven. Last one to Africa." Weaver tipped his chin toward Max. "You?"

RJ came by with the coffee and poured a cup for Max. "Anybody else?"

Weaver and Jake both nodded.

RJ grinned. "You're in luck. I brought extra cups." She laid them in front of them and poured steaming brew into them. She started to leave and then turned back. "Jake. Question for you."

He smiled up at her. "Shoot."

"Your friend Hank, he has a computer guru, doesn't he?" she asked, her eyes narrowing. "Guy named Swede?"

Jake nodded. "That's right. Anytime we need

something we just call him up and let him know, and he'll do his best to look it up for us. Why?"

RJ shrugged. "I might have something that I want them to look into."

"Just let me know, and I'll contact Hank or Swede. Or heck, I can give you Hank's number and you can call him yourself."

"He wouldn't mind?"

Jake shook his head. "No, Hank's a pretty good guy. He likes to help people."

"Thanks," RJ said. "If you could forward his number to me on your cellphone, I'll give him a call."

"I'll do it right now." He pulled out his cellphone, scrolled through his contacts and forwarded Hank's number to RJ's phone. "You should have it now."

She pulled her cellphone out of her pocket and glanced down. "Got it. Thanks." She smiled and left the men sitting at the table, heading back to the bar to return the coffee pot and collect another tray full of drinks for the guests.

Then Stover and Curry stepped through the front door of the Watering Hole.

Max glanced toward JoJo at the bar. Her gaze swept the people coming through the front entrance, and her smile tightened. The two men glanced around the room, probably looking for an empty table. None were available, but there were two chairs at the bar. Max had second thoughts about coming to the table with Jake and Weaver. He wished he'd stayed at the bar. As the politician and his aide settled onto stools, JoJo pushed her shoulders back, lifted her chin and said something to them. They must have placed their orders because she went to work getting them between filling another order for RJ.

Gunny looked through the window between the bar and the kitchen and yelled, "Order up!"

RJ hurried to get to the order and took it out to the table full of hungry patrons. It appeared to be a typical night at the Watering Hole, with one exception. JoJo seemed very tense. Her movements were stiff, her brow puckered.

Max pushed to his feet. "If you guys will excuse me, I think I'll go give JoJo and RJ a hand."

Jake looked up, his eyes wide. "Maybe I should go check with Gunny. He might need some help in the kitchen." He turned to Weaver.

The newest man on their team smiled. "I can do kitchen or waitstaff."

"Why don't you come do kitchen with us," Jake said. "You can get to know Gunny better."

Weaver nodded. "Gotcha. But if you guys get backed up out here, just let me know."

Max strode across the room to the bar and leaned across the counter. "Could you use a hand mixing drinks?"

She nodded. "I could use a hand back here so that I can help RJ deliver food and drinks to the tables."

"Show me where everything is," he said, "and I'll take over."

She lifted the countertop door and let him through. The space behind the counter was pretty tight. They bumped into each other several times as she showed him where everything was and how everything worked. Each time they bumped into each other, a shock of electricity ripped through him, and he wondered if it did the same with her. If her widened eyes were an indication, each contact impacted her as well.

Stover and his aide's gazes followed her every move.

After Max made a couple of drinks, JoJo was satisfied that he could succeed, and she slipped out from behind the bar. With a quick grin and a good luck, JoJo took a loaded tray and carried it over to the farthest table. Between mixing drinks, Max kept a close eye on JoJo to make sure nobody made any unwanted advances toward her. He also kept a lookout for Roy to make sure he didn't return to the bar.

"You doing okay back there?" RJ asked as she came back with empties and orders for new drinks.

He'd been struggling with one of the taps.

RJ grinned. "That one's a little bit sticky; you have to really work with it. Try wiggling it side to side, and then pulling back on it."

He did and the beer flowed freely.

"I'll take two of those," she said. "And a Jack Daniel's on the rocks." She handed him a slip of paper. "And if you could put that up there for Gunny. They want some food to go along with their drinks."

He passed the order ticket through the window to the kitchen staff. When he turned, RJ had already gone with the tray of beer and whiskey.

JoJo was back with another tray full of empties.

"Order up!" Gunny called out.

Max turned to retrieve the plates of food and set them on a large tray.

"I'll take that," said JoJo.

When she left again, he had a little lull between filling drinks and passing food orders back to Gunny.

Stover grinned. "Good thing we had KP duty on active."

Max would bet that the politician never pulled KP. He'd likely been a high-ranking officer when he'd retired. "Yes, sir," Max said. In actuality, he hadn't pulled KP since basic, and even then, only to help stack the trays. The Army had been much busier training him how to be a soldier and fight, rather than how to cook and clean up. He'd quickly gone from basic infantry to special operations and, finally, Green Beret.

"So, what's the story with Gunny?" Stover asked.

Max frowned. "Pardon me?"

"Is he collecting strays? With all these former

active duty folks…you'd think he was running a halfway house for the military."

Anger bubbled up inside Max.

Stover raised his hands. "Oh, I'm not trying to be mean or anything. Don't get me wrong, I think it's admirable what he's done, giving Ms. Ramirez a job when she got off active duty, and then to give your organization a place to call home? It's admirable."

"Gunny's a good man." Max's fists tightened on the tap. "Can I get you another beer, sir?" He didn't like talking about Gunny behind his back. The man had welcomed the Brotherhood Protectors into his business and into his home. He was a patriot who loved his country and loved the men and women who fought for it.

"No." Stover glanced down at this mug. "I think I've got enough here for right now."

His aide had turned on his stool and was looking out at the floor, his gaze following JoJo.

"Mr. Curry, can I get you something?" Max asked in an attempt to draw the man's attention away from JoJo.

"I'll take another." The man shoved his empty mug toward Max without turning around.

Something about the man didn't sit right with him, so he filled his mug full of foam and pushed it back to him.

Curry frowned down at the foam, but he lifted

the mug and sipped, careful not to get foam on his lip.

RJ set a tray with empty bottles on the counter. "Can I get you guys something to eat?" she asked.

"No, thank you," Stover said. "We were just having a drink before our reservation in Fool's Gold." He glanced down at his watch. "It's about time we go." He laid a twenty on the counter.

"You have your key to get into the lodge?" RJ asked.

The politician patted his shirt pocket. "Yes, ma'am, I do. We'll be quiet coming in. We might be a little late."

She nodded. "See you guys in the morning."

"The rest of my campaign staff will be here before noon."

"What time would you and your aide like to have breakfast?" RJ asked.

"Eight o'clock sound good?" Stover asked.

She nodded. "Eight o'clock, it is. See you then." She grabbed the tray filled with drinks and crossed the floor.

Stover and his aide slid off their stools and headed for the door. The aide eyed JoJo as he held the door for his boss.

Max's fists clenched. He didn't like the intensity with which the man stared at JoJo. Then he and the politician were gone. The rest of the evening was fill glasses, wash glasses, mix drinks and repeat. Until sometime after nine-thirty, when the working-class people headed home to get a good night's sleep before they had to start another day at work.

RJ and JoJo stacked chairs on tables and swept and mopped the floors. Max washed all the glasses, put them away and cleaned the floor and the countertop of the bar. Gunny, Jake and Weaver emerged from the kitchen.

"We're all done inside," Gunny said. "Anyone up for some coffee or hot cocoa in the lodge?"

JoJo shook her head. "No way. I'm beat. I'm going home to bed."

"I'll take you up on that hot cocoa," RJ said.

"Me, too," Jake said.

Weaver raised a hand. "Count me in as well."

"What about you, Max?" Gunny asked.

"I need to make a run to town. I won't be long."

JoJo glanced his direction but didn't say anything.

RJ locked the front door, and they all left through the back.

JoJo climbed into her car, waited until Gunny, RJ, Jake and Weaver had passed before pinning Max with, "Hey, you."

He'd expected her to stop him and argue about him following her home.

"Do you really need to go to town?" JoJo asked.

"Yes, I do."

"Why?" she asked with her arms crossed over her chest.

He grinned. "To make sure a certain person gets to her apartment all right, and that no one is lurking in the parking lot."

Her mouth formed a tight smile. "Sometimes, I wonder if you're not the stalker I need to worry about."

His grin faded, and he gave her a stern look. "I'm just concerned. Even though I know you can stick up for yourself, I like to know that you get home safely."

She opened her mouth to say something but then closed it. After a long pause she said, "Thank you. I appreciate it."

He tried not to show his surprise. The man in the vehicle the previous night must have scared her. Frankly, the incident scared him, too. Why would somebody be sitting outside her apartment most of the night? And was he the same person who had attempted to break in? "I'd sure feel better if you'd just stay here tonight."

She sighed. "I didn't bring any clothes, and I already told RJ that I wasn't staying."

"We can go to your apartment, get your clothes and come back. You can tell RJ that you felt like she'd really need the help in the morning. She doesn't have to know that you had a stalker last night outside your apartment."

"She's my friend. I hate to lie to her."

"Then tell her the truth—that you're going back to

your apartment to get your stuff because you had somebody lurking outside your apartment."

JoJo's lips twisted. "She'd have me moved in here permanently."

Max cocked an eyebrow. "And is that such a bad thing?"

JoJo frowned. "I've always been surrounded by people. I need to learn how to live on my own."

"Why?" Max asked.

She squared her shoulders and lifted her chin. "I just do. I can't be afraid to go to sleep at night."

"Well, when you have somebody trying to get into your apartment, you better damn well be afraid."

She chuckled. "Okay, I'll go get my clothes and come right back, but you don't have to follow me."

"The hell I don't. Better yet, why don't you ride with me? That way, whoever is watching won't know it's you until after you've gotten your stuff, gotten back into my vehicle, and we're on our way back to the lodge."

Her lips twisted. "I hate relying on you."

"I hate that you hate that." He crossed his arms over his chest, "So, what's it gonna be?"

She said, "I'll go with you."

"Great. Come on." He held her car door for her. She climbed out, and they walked together to his truck.

Max helped her up into the passenger seat.

JoJo laughed. "I need a ladder to get up into this monster."

"I can't help it that you're short."

"Watch it, buddy. I might be short, but I'm tough."

He grinned up at her. "Boy, don't I know," and he rubbed the back of his neck with a grin.

"I said I was sorry," she said.

"Hey, I'm gonna milk it for all the embarrassment it caused me."

"Seems I hurt your ego more than I hurt the back of your head."

"Got that right." Max climbed into the driver's seat, started the truck and pulled out of the parking lot and into the road headed toward Fool's Gold.

It didn't take long to reach her apartment.

"I'll only be a few minutes," she said.

He shook his head. "Nope. I'm going with you."

"I think I can gather my own clothes. I don't need any help to do that."

"And what if whoever tried to get into your apartment last night succeeded today and is waiting for you?" Max raised his eyebrows and waited for her response.

Her frown deepened. "I'll hear him and, if I have to, I'll shoot him. My gun's in the nightstand and my mace is on top of it."

"Do you have your concealed carry?" Max asked.

She nodded. "I do."

"Why aren't you carrying?"

"I didn't think I'd need it out at the lodge, just in my apartment at night."

"You should have it on you at all times."

She bit her lip and stared at the road ahead. "I hate it when you're right."

He grinned and walked with her up to her apartment.

Max inspected the doorframe, where it appeared someone had indeed taken something sharp to the wood around the lock. Fortunately, the deadbolt had held true.

"Let me go in first," he said.

"I went to basic combat training, too," she said.

He sighed. "But was that your job in the Army?"

"It could've been. Motor pool mechanics have to clear a building." Her lips twisted. "Fine. You go first."

"Thank you." He pulled his weapon out from beneath his jacket.

"Whoa," JoJo's eyes widened. "I didn't know you were carrying."

"I have my concealed carry, and I use it. This baby goes with me everywhere. Open the door and then wait here. I'll be right back."

JoJo unlocked the door then stood to the side.

Max pushed open the door and started to step inside when the smell of rotten eggs hit him. His hand froze on the doorknob, and his heart stopped for a full second. "Get back," he said.

"What?" JoJo frowned. "I still need my clothes."

"Get back now," he said, his tone harsh. "Go back down to the truck."

"What's wrong?" she asked.

"Gas." He eased the door closed, careful not to make the metal strike the metal latch.

JoJo ran out into the parking lot, pulled her cellphone out and called 911.

As Max stepped away from the apartment building, a huge explosion erupted, flinging him to the pavement.

CHAPTER 10

MAX HIT the ground hard enough that it knocked the breath out of him and made his ears ring. Debris rained down on him, and he covered his head with his hands.

As soon as he could breathe again, he got to his hands and knees and looked for JoJo. She was flat on her back on the ground, her cellphone lying a few feet away. Max's ears rang, and every sound came to him as if from the end of a very long tunnel. He crawled across the pavement to JoJo.

"Hey, JoJo," he said, his voice echoing in his ears. "JoJo, sweetheart."

She blinked her eyes open and stared up at him. "What happened?"

"An explosion. Stay here. I want to make sure there aren't other people in the apartments next to yours."

"It was in my apartment?" She pushed to a sitting position and reached for her cellphone.

"Yes, get in my truck and stay there."

She shook her head, and then swayed. "No, I'm going with you. If there are people in there, we need to get them out."

Knowing he couldn't hold her back, Max held out his hand, drew JoJo to her feet and made sure she could stand before he pulled his cellphone out of his pocket and dialed 911.

"I was doing that when my apartment exploded." She rubbed the back of her head. "Now, I know how you felt."

He gave the information to the dispatcher then ran toward the building. He headed for the apartment next door to JoJo's. Before he reached the door, a man jerked it open and staggered out, wearing nothing but boxer shorts, his hair dusted with sheetrock.

"What the hell happened?" he said.

"Gas leak explosion," Max responded. "Is there anyone else in your apartment?"

The man shook his head. "No."

"Stay out of the building while I check the rest of the apartments," he said.

JoJo joined him as he went to the door of the apartment on the other side of hers. "Last I knew, this one was empty," she said. "I haven't kept up to make sure."

Max banged on the door. No one responded. He banged again. Sirens could be heard in the distance, the volume increasing as fire and emergency vehicles neared the apartment complex. Max tried kicking in the door. He couldn't do it with his bum leg, but he had to balance on his bad leg if he wanted to kick with the other one. He just didn't have the strength to break the door in with a kick.

By then, the other residents of the apartment were coming out of theirs, farther away from JoJo's unit. They emerged in the dark, wearing their pajamas or bathrobes. An officer's vehicle pulled up, followed by a firetruck and an ambulance. Max met the sheriff as he got out of his vehicle and explained what had happened.

"You guys need to see the emergency medical technician and make sure you're okay and don't have concussions." The sheriff pointed to the waiting ambulance. "Go."

Max nodded and took JoJo over to the ambulance where the EMT checked them out. He said they didn't appear to have concussions. However, they would be well advised to go to the local hospital anyway and have an emergency room doctor check them out. He told them he'd gladly load them in the ambulance and take them there.

JoJo shook her head. "No, I don't need that. I'm going to go back out to the lodge."

Max said, "You really need to go to the hospital

and have them check you out. You landed hard on the back of your head."

Her lips pouted. "I just want to get out to the lodge."

"Will you do it for me, please? I promise I'll take you there and take you back out to the lodge immediately after."

She pinched the bridge of her nose. "If my head didn't hurt so bad, I'd say hell no, take me to the lodge now. Fine. I'll go to the hospital."

Max helped her into his truck. He told the sheriff where they'd be after they were finished at the hospital, and then they left. When they arrived at the emergency room of the little hospital in Fool's Gold, he parked at the entrance and walked her in. Max handed her off to the nurse, and then went to park the truck.

He was back as quickly as he could manage. But by then, they'd already taken JoJo back to an examination room.

"I'd like to see Ms. Ramirez," he said.

"Are you a relative?" the clerk at the desk asked.

He frowned. "No, I'm not." He just wanted to see JoJo.

The woman shook her head. "I'm sorry, sir, you can't go back."

"But I brought her here," he said.

"I'm sorry, sir, those are the rules." The clerk

raised her eyebrows. "Now, if you were her fiancé, we would be able to let you back."

"In that case, I am her fiancé," he said.

The nurses eyes narrowed. "And if I ask the young lady if she has a fiancé, will she say she does?"

Max started to nod, and then shook his head. "Mmm maybe not, because I haven't popped the question yet. If you'll let me go back there, I will."

The woman tilted her head to the side, her eyes narrowing. "Mmm, I don't know."

"Please," he said, "all she has to do is say yes, and she's my fiancé."

"Why am I just not buying this?" the woman said.

"Please. Let me give it a shot," he said.

"First, answer a few questions." The clerk tapped a pencil on the clean white pad of paper. "What's her favorite color?"

Max almost gave up then, instead, he said, "Blue."

"Her favorite football team?"

"Dallas Cowboys."

The clerk rose from her desk and went through a door behind the counter. "Give me a minute. I'll go ask her if she wants you back there. And if her answers to those questions are right, I'll let you come back and do your proposal. It'll be our first in the emergency room."

Max paced as the clerk went back. He imagined what JoJo's response would be to the questions and to the idea that he was her fiancé. All he wanted was to make sure that she was okay. He needed to see her, to know for certain. Then he wouldn't leave her alone for a second.

A few minutes later, the restricted doors opened, and the clerk waved toward him. "You can come in."

He hesitated. "Seriously? I got the answers to the questions right?"

The nurse shook her head. "No."

"Her favorite color isn't blue?" Max asked.

"It's orange. The color of the sunset," the nurse said, "And her favorite football team is the Denver Broncos."

Max frowned. "Then why are you letting me go back?"

"Because when I asked her if she had a fiancé, she looked surprised."

"Again, why are you letting me go back?"

"Because when I told her that you were going to propose back here, she smiled. When I asked her if I could bring you back, she said yes, and she wants to see you get down on your knee. So, come on Romeo, the entire staff is waiting for you to ask her."

Max almost turned and left, but he was more concerned about seeing that JoJo was okay. If it meant he had to go down on one knee and propose, so be it. She'd likely say, *oh hell, no*, and the nurses would boot him out. But at least he'd have seen that she was okay. So, he followed the clerk and found what seemed like the entire staff of the hospital lining the hallway outside an examination room.

A nurse waved her hand toward the door. "Ms. Ramirez is waiting."

When he stepped inside, Max found JoJo sitting up on the hospital bed, a smile playing at her lips.

With his audience watching and some of them with their cellphones out taking video images, Max did the only thing he could. He got down on one knee. "JoJo, sweetheart, you're an amazing woman. So brave, so mechanically talented, and beautiful..." Under the pressure of a dozen eyes watching him, he took a deep breath and asked, "Will you marry me?"

Her eyes widened, and she whispered, "I didn't think you'd actually do it."

He frowned and glanced right and left at the different people standing watching them. "That's not much of an answer. They're going to kick me out if you don't say yes."

"In that case, Max, I'll be your one and only mechanic."

He shook his head. "I don't think that was the answer these people are looking for and neither am I."

"Fine," she said, "Yes, I'll marry you."

"Kiss the bride," the clerk said.

"I don't know," Max said. "She's been injured."

"She's not so badly injured if she can say yes. You

can at least kiss her very gently if nothing else," a nurse said.

The half a dozen people standing around watching clapped and cheered.

A man in a white coat came into the room. "Did I miss something?"

The nurse grinned. "Only our first proposal in the ER."

"Is that right?" The doctor grinned. "Let me guess, head injury?"

JoJo frowned. "Yes. Why do you say it that way?"

He turned to Max, "Don't be surprised if she has no memory of this proposal tomorrow."

"Ya think?" Max said.

"Well, if she wanted it, she'll remember it. If she didn't want it, she'll conveniently forget." He winked at JoJo. "And if you need a doctor's excuse to forget, just let me know." He shined a light into both of her eyes, checked the lump on the back of her head and told her to get some rest. Otherwise, she was released from the hospital.

"Thank you, doctor," JoJo said. As she started to get up off the bed, the doctor held up his hand. "Sorry, you can't walk out on your own. You have to go out in a wheelchair."

"But I feel fine," JoJo insisted. "I can walk. See?"

"Hospital rules," a nurse said as she wheeled a chair into the room. "Consider yourself lucky you get to go home tonight."

JoJo slid off the table and into the wheelchair.

Max almost laughed at the disgusted look on her face. "Don't worry, sweetheart. It won't be long before you're home."

"I'm counting on that," JoJo said.

"Come on, my little fiancée, let's get you out of here." He strode alongside her as the nurse pushed the wheelchair to the exit. Max left her at the door as he went to get the truck and pull it around in front of the ER. He parked and got out to help JoJo up into the seat.

As he helped buckle her seatbelt, he whispered, "Are you doing okay?"

She nodded. "I am."

"Let's get you back to the lodge before Gunny sends out a posse to find you. Knowing his network, he's probably already heard about the explosion at your apartment building."

"I hope not," JoJo said. "He'll be worried. I have to admit, I'm worried."

"I can't believe that was an accident," Max said.

"You think someone set it up to explode?" JoJo asked.

"Based on the fact that somebody tried to get into your apartment sometime early this morning, and then to have your gas have a leak on the same day…?" Max shook his head. "It's too coincidental. I don't believe in coincidences."

JoJo looked down at her hands then back up at

him. "If you hadn't come with me tonight, I could've been dead. Why?" JoJo asked. "Who would want to kill me?"

"The question is, who have you pissed off? All I can think of is Roy, but I can't imagine somebody like Roy going to the trouble of creating a gas leak in your apartment. I don't think he's that smart. Have you made anybody else mad recently?"

"No," she said, "but I have an idea."

Max waited. When she didn't expand, he said, "And that idea would be what?"

"It's not something I want to discuss," she said.

"If it involves risking your life, I would hope that you would discuss it with me or somebody else who can help you."

She nodded. "And I will, when I'm ready."

"Well, I hope you're ready before this guy gets to you and kills you."

"Me, too," she said. "Me, too."

CHAPTER 11

JoJo had vowed that she would never rely on a man again but, if not for Max, she would be dead. Since she'd met him, he'd been nothing but a gentleman. He had been protective without being possessive, but mostly, he'd been there when she'd needed him. And though she hated the fact that she needed him, she didn't hate him.

When they arrived at Lost Valley Ranch, the place was lit up like the Fourth of July. Lights streamed from inside and every porch light shined brightly. Max had barely parked the car when everybody came out of the lodge at once, RJ leading the way. She engulfed JoJo in a huge hug, holding her as tightly as she could.

JoJo laughed breathlessly. "I guess you heard?"

"Yes." RJ held her at arm's length. "I couldn't believe it. Your apartment exploded?"

"If it hadn't been for Max…" JoJo shot a glance toward the man.

Jake shook hands with Max. "You okay, buddy?"

Max nodded. "Other than a little residual ringing in the ears, I'm fine."

"You were lucky," Gunny said. "I talked to the sheriff. He said the apartment was pretty much destroyed."

"Everything I owned was in that apartment." JoJo snorted softly. "Not that it was much."

"Don't you worry about it," RJ said. "We'll take care of you."

JoJo frowned. "So much for taking care of myself."

"You're alive, aren't you?" RJ said. "I've got some clothes you can wear. They might be big on you, but you can wear them until we can get you to Colorado Springs to do some shopping." She squeezed JoJo's arms and gave her a crooked smile. "Can't think of a better excuse to go shopping."

JoJo shook her head. "But we don't have time. We've got the campaign staff event this weekend."

RJ stood back and looked at JoJo. "You know, I think you and Emily might be the same height. I'll ask her if she can bring some things out for you when she comes tomorrow. Next week, we'll plan a shopping trip. Did you have renter's insurance?"

JoJo nodded. "I did. It wasn't much, but then I didn't have much."

"We'll get in touch with the insurance company

tomorrow and see what we can get. It'll at least be a start. In the meantime, you're staying here at the lodge as long as you need to." RJ hugged JoJo again. "I'm just thankful you're alive." She reached out a hand to Max. "Thank you for being there for her."

"And to think I didn't want him to follow me," JoJo said, shaking her head.

"Come on. Let's get you inside." RJ herded her toward the front door like a mother hen. "I'm sure you're ready for bed."

JoJo nodded. "And we have an early morning tomorrow."

RJ shook her head. "Not for you. You can sleep in."

JoJo's brow knit. "Since when have I ever slept in?"

"Since you got knocked flat on your ass and you need to." RJ shrugged. "Whatever, let's at least get you to bed so you can get *some* sleep."

Stover and Curry stepped out on the porch.

"What's all the commotion?" Stover asked.

"Nothing for you to worry about," Gunny said.

Curry frowned. "What's this I hear about an explosion?"

Gunny glance toward the man. "Where'd you hear about that?"

"We heard it over the radio," Stover said. "I like to dial into the police scanner. It gives me a good idea of what's going on in the area and what kinds of crimes are prevalent. I'm glad to see you two are all right. Were there any other casualties?"

JoJo shook her head. "No, thank goodness. Just some shaken residents."

"Did the fire chief give you any idea what caused the explosion?" Currie asked.

"They're going to conduct an investigation," Max said. "But I smelled rotten eggs. There was a gas leak somewhere."

"You would think that the building regulations in an apartment complex would keep that from happening," Stover said.

Max's eyes narrowed. "Unless somebody *wanted* it to happen."

Stover's eyebrows rose. "You think the explosion was intentional? That somebody caused that leak?"

JoJo met Max's gaze. "We don't know what to think. We're going to let the fire chief do his investigation and determine the cause."

"In the meantime," RJ said, "JoJo is staying with us."

"Do you have enough rooms for her and the rest of my staff?" Stover asked. "Because if you don't, I can put some of my people up at the casino."

"No, we'll have enough room," RJ said. "We have one other person coming out to help tomorrow. She can bunk with me when she arrives." RJ slipped an arm around JoJo's waist. "Come on, let's get you upstairs." RJ looked over her shoulder at Gunny. "I don't suppose you'd make a cup of hot cocoa for JoJo...?"

Gunny's forehead wrinkled. "You bet I can. Anything for my girls." He leaned in and gave JoJo a big hug. "I'm glad you're okay, and I'm glad you're staying with us." He turned to the rest and said, "Okay, people. Show's over. We have a busy day tomorrow. Let's hit the sack."

RJ walked JoJo up the stairs. "I put you in the room next to mine. You'll be in between me and Max. If you want to bunk with me, I'd be happy to have you in my room."

JoJo shook her head. "I'd rather not disturb you in the night. After what happened today, I don't know what's going to happen tonight in my dreams."

RJ nodded. "Well, there are connecting doors between your room and mine and your room and Max's. If you need either one of us, just knock on the door." RJ led her down the hall and pushed a door open. "So, you can stay in here for as long as you'd like. Sadly, you'll have to share the bathroom with me, Max and Jake. It's across the hall. We're all pretty quick, so it shouldn't be too much of a problem. There are fresh towels in there. I'm sure you're going to want to use the bathroom to shower all of the dust off of you."

JoJo sighed. "I hate this."

"Oh, sweetie." RJ stared down at her. "Why?"

"I didn't want to be a burden on anybody," JoJo said.

RJ hugged her. "You're never a burden. You're family. You're the sister I always wanted. You're here most of the time anyway, so you might as well stay the nights."

"You and Gunny have done so much for me. I owe you guys so much."

"You don't owe us anything. We're blessed that you're a part of our family and our lives. Now, you head off to the bathroom. I'll bring you some fresh night clothes and something to wear for tomorrow. And if you give me the clothes you're wearing now, I'll get those washed tonight so that you'll have them for whenever you need them."

"Thank you, RJ," JoJo said, tears welling in her eyes.

RJ had matching tears. "I just wonder what our lives would've been like had we been able to fulfill our plan and both of us go into the military at the same time. Somehow, I feel responsible for what happened to you because I wasn't there to protect you."

JoJo shook her head. "No, no, no, RJ, you cannot even begin to feel responsible for what happened to me. You weren't even there."

"Yes, but I should have been."

"Maybe it was all fate, and this was all supposed to happen to me."

RJ squeezed her eyes shut. "Then fate can be a huge pain in the ass."

JoJo grinned. "You know the saying, what doesn't kill you makes you stronger."

RJ's laughter choked on a sob. "Now that's not funny."

"No, but I've got to believe that everything happens for a reason. Maybe the reason why it happened to me, and I lived, is so that I could bring this person to justice who could be doing the same thing to other women."

"All the more reason for you to let me talk to Hank and see if his guy Swede can dig up anything about the investigation, the people on that base or anything else that might help nail that bastard."

JoJo's lips pressed together tightly. She drew in a deep breath through her nose and blew it out through her mouth. "Okay, let's let him dig in."

RJ smiled. "Good. I've got his number. I'll give him a call tonight."

JoJo shook her head. "This late?"

"From what Jake tells me about Hank, he doesn't care what time you call him. If you need something, he's there for you."

"I'd like to meet that man," JoJo said.

"I think you eventually will. I can't imagine him setting up shop here in Colorado and not coming down to visit his team here." RJ stood back. "Now, go. Get your shower. I'll slip some clothes inside the door. And if you don't feel up to going downstairs for the cocoa, I'll bring it up to you."

"Don't do that. I can go down."

"Good, because I'm feeling kind of snack-ish. I think I'm going to make a sandwich, too. Do you want half a sandwich with me?"

JoJo nodded. "Sounds good." With nothing of her own to take with her, JoJo walked across the hall and entered the bathroom. After she closed the door, she leaned against the wood panels. Everything that had happened to her hit her like a tsunami, and a sob rose up her throat. A soft knock sounded at the door. JoJo scrubbed the tears from her face and swallowed hard on the lump lodged in her throat. She turned to open the door, expecting to see RJ standing there with a handful of clothes. Instead, it was Max.

"Hey," he said, "are you all right?"

She tried to keep it together, but she couldn't. The tears welling in her eyes spilled down her cheeks.

He opened his arms. "I'm not pushing this, but if you want me to hold you…"

JoJo fell into his arms and buried her cheek against his chest. She sobbed quietly, standing there in the hallway barely aware of when RJ stepped around them to put clothes inside on the counter in the bathroom. She didn't say a word but disappeared. JoJo stood in the shelter of Max's arms for how long she didn't know. All she did know was that was the only place where she felt safe.

When her sobs subsided, he tipped her chin up with his finger and brushed a thumb across her cheek, wiping away some of the tears.

"I don't know what's wrong with me," JoJo said. "I never cry. It seems I've cried more in these last couple of days than I have my entire life. Even after I woke up in the dirt in the desert, I didn't cry this much."

"There's no shame in tears," he said. "Maybe it's your body's way of letting go of the hurt and anger. In that case, cry all you can."

She shook her head. "I need the anger. It's the fuel I need to find the man who did this to me. Now, it seems I need to find the man who destroyed my apartment tonight." She looked up through her tear-washed eyes and into Max's. "Could they be the same person?"

Max frowned. "The same person as who?"

JoJo went on as if he hadn't asked a question. "The people who were on that base where I was deployed to have to be back in the States by now. It's a scary thought, but it could be the same person." JoJo's jaw hardened and her eyes narrowed. "I hope the hell it is."

Max's frown deepened. "Not sure what you're talking about, JoJo."

She continued. "If it is him, I hope he comes after me again. It might be the only way to find him."

"Whoever it is seems pretty determined to get to you. I mean, if he tried to get into your apartment and couldn't, and then came back and did...he's persistent." He frowned down at her. "Promise me something."

"What?" she asked.

He swept a strand of her hair back from her forehead and tucked it behind her ear. "Promise me you won't go anywhere without me."

She laughed. "I can't tie up all of your time chasing after me. You have a life. Potentially, you'll have other assignments. We have no idea how long this will go on."

"To hell with my life and assignments. I'm worried about *your* life." He brushed another tear with his thumb and lowered that same thumb to brush it across her lips. "I'm worried about you." He frowned and started to pull his hand away. "But maybe, that's not what you want to hear."

JoJo caught his wrist and turned her face to press her lips into his palm. His hands were so strong and yet so gentle. After the attack that had left her nearly dead, she'd thought she'd never want another man to touch her. But then she hadn't known Max.

He kissed her forehead. "Get your shower. Gunny's got some hot chocolate ready for you downstairs. I'm going to get a shower after you."

She nodded and stepped away, feeling very bereft without his strong arms around her. JoJo entered the bathroom, closed the door and turned on the shower. She stripped out of her clothes and studied herself in the mirror. Other than a few cuts and scrapes, she was all right. They were just surface wounds. It was the wounds in her mind and heart she struggled with most.

The gentleness of Max's kiss on her forehead gave her hope.

JoJo climbed into the shower and rinsed the dust and grit from her body. She washed her hair, applied conditioner and rinsed quickly. Knowing Max would be in there next, she didn't take too long.

RJ had left pajamas, a robe and a cute pair of lacy pink underwear on the counter. JoJo stepped into the items and smiled at her reflection in the mirror. RJ was a good five or six inches taller than JoJo. The legs and arms of the pajamas were too long, but JoJo was glad to have them.

She rolled up the sleeves and the pantlegs, slipped the robe over her shoulders and tied it around her waist. The ever-thoughtful RJ had left a brush on the counter as well. JoJo eased the tangles out of her hair. When she was done, she felt a little closer to normal. She stepped out of the bathroom and found Max leaning against the wall, his shaving kit in his hand.

JoJo smiled. "It's all yours."

"Thanks. I'll be down in a minute." He frowned.

"Unless you want to wait in your room until I'm done and can go down with you."

With a twisted grin, she shook her head. "I think I'll be fine by myself in the lodge. I'll see you downstairs." JoJo carried her dirty clothes down the stairs to the laundry room near the kitchen, dropping her clothes in a basket. She entered the kitchen to find Gunny, RJ, Jake and Cage Weaver busy making sandwiches and hot chocolate.

She smiled. "Glad I found the party."

"You're just in time," Gunny said. He poured hot cocoa from a pan into a mug. "Careful, it's hot." He pointed to some bowls on the counter. "Put what you want in it."

JoJo grinned. "It's like old times, isn't it?"

RJ smiled. "Gunny always knows how to make hot chocolate interesting, doesn't he?"

JoJo couldn't decide between all the bowls of toppings that she could put into her hot cocoa. She started with crushed candy canes to give it a peppermint flavor, added a pinch of cayenne to give it a little kick, then she squirted a little chocolate syrup in and dropped a handful of mini marshmallows on top. She wrapped her hands around the mug, enjoying the warmth. As she waited for it to cool enough so that she could take a sip, she watched as the others worked.

RJ sliced a sandwich in half and laid it on a platter with a dozen other sandwiches.

JoJo laughed. "You'd think we were feeding an army."

RJ rolled her eyes. "You ought to see these guys eat. They have stomachs like teenage boys."

"I wish," Jake said. "It was a lot easier to keep a sixpack back then." He patted his flat belly. "Right now, I'm working on a keg."

RJ rolled her eyes. "As if. You don't have an ounce of fat on you."

He slipped his arms around her and pulled her back against his front. "That won't be the case if you keep feeding me this way."

She leaned into him, a sweet smile on her face.

JoJo was happy for her friend.

Gunny poured the rest of the hot cocoa into mugs and laid the mugs on a tray. When he was done, Weaver stepped up.

"I'll take the cocoa into the dining room," Weaver said.

"Good," Gunny said. "I'll get the toppings and bring them in." He set all the bowls on a tray and fished a can of whipped topping out of the refrigerator. Jake took the platter of sandwiches, and RJ went to the cupboard and pulled out several bags of potato chips in a variety of flavors.

"Now that you've got it all taken care of," JoJo said, "what can I do to help?"

Gunny grinned. "Just come in and sit down. We'll enjoy your company."

They arranged the food and drinks on a buffet in the dining room, but once they had their cups and sandwiches, they adjourned to the great room and settled onto the large bomber-jacket-brown leather couches. Gunny stirred up the fire in the fireplace and added a log.

By that time, Max came down the stairs and helped himself to a mug of cocoa, squirting the whipped topping across the top of it.

JoJo settled on a loveseat, whether subconsciously hoping that Max would sit beside her, she didn't know, but he did. She smiled at the big dollop of whipped cream on top of his cocoa. "Never would have taken you for a whipped cream kind of guy."

He grinned. "Told you I had a sweet tooth."

"I thought you were making that up just so you could follow me into town." She took a careful sip of her hot cocoa.

"I did. I had plenty of peppermints, but it gave me a good excuse to follow you into town, didn't it?"

She shook her head and took another tentative sip of her drink.

Curry and Stover came in from outside.

Gunny tipped his head toward the dining room. "You guys, help yourself to the cocoa on the buffet and come join us."

Maybe it was selfish of JoJo, but she really didn't want the politician and his aide to join them in the great room. She liked the current composition of the gathering just the way it was.

"I don't suppose you have some coffee?" Stover asked.

"As a matter of fact, I do," Gunny said. "Here, let me get it for you."

"If you'll just tell me where it is, I'll get it myself," Stover said.

"Easier to show you than tell you." Gunny walked with the man to the kitchen.

Miles Curry helped himself to the cocoa bar and took a seat in the dining room on the edge of the great room.

JoJo was glad that Max was sitting between her and Curry. Stover's aide had an odd way of looking at people, as if he were studying them under a microscope. Was he looking for their weaknesses?

JoJo shook her head. Once again, she was reading into traits that might not even be there.

Gunny and Stover returned, and Stover took his seat next to Curry at the dining table on the edge of the great room. Curry pulled out a computer tablet and propped it up in front of Stover. They put their heads together and talked softly between them.

RJ brought JoJo half a sandwich. "It's your favorite. Swiss cheese and pastrami."

JoJo smiled up at RJ. "You're going to spoil me."

"Only if you let me." RJ perched on the edge of

JoJo's couch and leaned close to JoJo's ear. "I spoke to Hank," she whispered.

JoJo shot a look up at her. "And?"

"And he said he'd check into it."

"Thanks," JoJo said. RJ's news should've given her some sense of relief. Instead, it made her tense.

Max must have felt her stiffening beside him. He held out his hand palm up.

Without hesitation, she placed her hand in his. He closed his fingers around hers gently. That little bit of reassurance went a long way. She relaxed a little and sipped her hot cocoa, sucking one of the little marshmallows into her mouth. It reminded her of a time long ago when she and RJ would sit up until late into the night in RJ's bedroom with their hot cocoa that Gunny had made from scratch. RJ may not have grown up with her mother, but Gunny had done everything in his power, and in his Marine way, to give her a happy childhood.

Having been raised by a single mom, JoJo understood the difficulties of single parenthood that Gunny had faced. Only it was worse for Gunny because he'd had to occasionally deploy. Which meant that RJ spent time living with her grandparents while her father fought on the other side of the world for twelve to fourteen months at a time.

JoJo had felt lucky that her mother wasn't active military, but she still hadn't seen much of her mother because the woman had to work two jobs just to put enough money in their accounts to pay the rent and put food on the table, which made JoJo a latchkey child.

She'd learned to cook meals at the age of nine, and she'd taken care of all the household chores, including washing dishes, laundry and mopping floors. But when her chores were done, she was allowed to escape to RJ's house, where she, too, was a latchkey child when Gunny had to work long hours.

They'd formed a special bond during their teenage years. JoJo valued her friendship with RJ, and she loved that Gunny had taken her in when her own mother had died in a car wreck coming back from her second job, right before their high school graduation. Gunny and RJ had seen her through some of the worst days of her life with the sudden passing of her mother. She didn't know what she would've done if she hadn't had them to hold her up. And once again, they were holding her up.

RJ sat next to Jake on one of the other leather sofas.

Jake sipped on his hot cocoa and looked over the top of his mug at Max. "I called Hank and let him know what was going on. He said that if you really think that someone is out to harm JoJo, she should be your first assignment."

Max's hand tightened on JoJo's. "What do you mean?"

JoJo frowned. "Yeah, what do you mean?"

Jake stared across the room at JoJo, his expression serious. "The purpose of the Brotherhood Protectors is to do just that...to protect."

"Kind of figured that, based on the name," JoJo said. "But why me? I'm not a paying customer. There's no way I can afford a bodyguard, no matter how reasonable he might be."

"When I came on board just a couple of weeks ago, I didn't know what to expect. Hank had sent one of his guys, Kujo, out to recruit and to set up shop here in Colorado. When Kujo came knocking at my door I didn't know what to think. I wasn't sure exactly what they had in mind for me, and since I didn't have any other job offers lined up for a one-legged man, I thought, what the heck? When RJ was targeted, Kujo and Hank decided that I needed to prove my salt with RJ. My job was to protect her." A grin spread across his face, and he turned to RJ.

RJ returned his smile with one of her own. "I probably wouldn't be alive today if it hadn't been for Hank and Kujo assigning Jake to protect me." She glanced across at JoJo and Max. "I think it's a great idea that Max's first assignment is to protect JoJo."

JoJo pulled her hand free of Max's and frowned. "I don't think I like the idea of being someone's assignment."

"If you're being targeted," RJ said, "you need somebody to watch your back. I was like you. I thought I could take care of myself. I didn't think I needed Jake to keep me safe. I was proven wrong. It really does help to have somebody else have your back," RJ said. "Let Max help you."

JoJo wasn't sure she liked the idea of Max being her assigned bodyguard. He'd pretty much been protecting her since the beginning, but that had been out of the goodness of his own heart, not as his assignment. How would he feel about her if she was only his assignment? And why did she care? He had already proven resourceful while protecting her. Then again, somebody seemed to be out to get her. She needed someone to help keep her safe.

Max glanced her way. "What do you say?"

JoJo shrugged. "Whatever."

Jake clapped his hands together. "Good. Then it's settled. Max will be JoJo's security."

JoJo pushed to her feet. "Well then, let me make it easy on you, I'm going to bed. You can have the night off." She carried her mug into the kitchen and rinsed it out in the sink. The swinging door squeaked on its hinges, indicating somebody had come into the kitchen behind her. She turned to find Max carrying his mug in as well. He rinsed it and put it in the dishwasher.

"You don't have to call it a night on my account," JoJo said.

Max shook his head. "I don't know about you, but I'm tired. It's not every day that you get blown up." He gave her twisted grin. "How are you feeling?"

"I have a little bit of a headache," she admitted. "And my tailbone is a little bit sore from landing on it. Other than that, I'm all right. What about you?" she asked, her brow furrowing. "You were closer to the explosion than I was."

Max pressed his palm to his left ear. "Still have a little ringing in my ear. And everybody seems to be talking as if from the far end of a tunnel, but I'm okay."

She nodded. "I'm glad you weren't hurt any worse than that. That explosion could've ended much worse for both of us."

He held out his hand. "Ready to call it a night?"

JoJo laid her hand in his, liking the way it felt. "Past ready."

They left the kitchen and walked back through the great room.

The others were gathering up the items from the hot cocoa bar.

"Goodnight," RJ called out as they passed by.

"*Buenos Noches*," JoJo said and started up the stairs with Max beside her.

When they reached her room, Max's grip on her hand tightened. "JoJo."

She stopped with her free hand reaching for the door, her heart fluttering in her chest. He'd kissed her forehead earlier; would he do it again? Did she want him to? Or did she want him to kiss her lips? "Yes, Max?"

"I don't want you to feel uncomfortable, but I'd feel a whole lot better if you left the connecting door between our rooms opened or unlocked.

"You think somebody will attack me here?"

"After what happened today, I don't want to risk it. Look, you don't have to," he said, "but think about it."

She nodded. "I'll think about it." She entered her room and turned in the threshold before she closed the door, "Max?"

"Yes, JoJo?"

She came back out of the room, leaned up on her tiptoes and pressed a kiss to his lips. "Thank you for saving me today."

He raised a hand to cup her cheek. "It was my pleasure." He bent to press his lips to her forehead, only JoJo moved, tipping her head back to capture his mouth with hers.

His lips were soft but firm against hers and every bit as wonderful as she'd imagined. Her pulse quickened, but not out of fear. She stepped closer until her body touched his.

Max gently cupped the back of her head and deepened the kiss.

When she opened to him, he swept in, sliding his tongue along hers.

Max broke the kiss first, stepped back and let his hands fall to his sides. "I am almost certain kissing the client is not part of the job." His lips twisted. "Go to bed, JoJo." He reached around her and pushed her door open.

She stepped inside and closed the door behind her. Her cheeks were hot, and her lips tingled. Hell, her entire body tingled. Not only had Max given her hope for a future relationship, but he'd also given her desire.

CHAPTER 12

MAX WAITED to hear the click of the lock on JoJo's door before he turned to enter his own room. He paced the short length of the floor from the door to the window several times, too anxious to sleep.

The gas leak in JoJo's apartment had been no accident. It had to have been arranged. Set up by somebody. Probably the one who had been lurking around her apartment the night before and had tried to get in. He wished he had confronted the man when he'd had a chance instead of just intimidating him into leaving.

At least she was under the same roof as he was, which gave him a better chance of keeping an eye on her. And now that she was his responsibility, his job, his assignment, her safety was his number one priority, and he shouldn't be kissing her. Not when she was now his client.

Max almost wished that Hank hadn't assigned him to her, because he sure wanted to kiss her again. He kicked off his shoes, slipped out of his jeans and tossed his T-shirt over the back of a chair. Though he wasn't sleepy, he lay down on top of the covers in his boxer shorts. Cocking his head toward the adjoining room, he strained to hear any sounds of movement, hoping to hear the sound of the lock turning in the connecting door between the two rooms. Either it was a very silent lock, or JoJo hadn't unlocked it. He laid with his hands laced behind his neck, staring up at the ceiling and the starlight coming through the window.

Kissing JoJo had been as natural as breathing, only a heck of a lot more exciting. He wanted to do it again. He was surprised that she had initiated it, as skittish as she'd been. He must have fallen asleep because the next thing he knew he heard someone calling out. It jerked him awake, and he sat up.

A muffled scream had him leaping out of bed and racing for the connecting door between his room and JoJo's. He prayed she had unlocked it. When he tried the door handle, it opened. He pushed it inward and called out softly, "JoJo?" He heard her moaning and sobbing. The sound was so heart wrenching, it made his chest tighten. He hurried toward her.

She lay in her bed writhing in the sheets. The comforter had fallen to the ground. The sheet had twisted around her body, keeping her from moving freely.

"No," she murmured. "No. Please, someone help me."

After having been tossed in the barn, Max was hesitant to touch her. JoJo's defensive reflex was in good order when she was awake. He wasn't sure how she'd react in her sleep.

"JoJo," he called out, "wake up."

Her head twisted back and forth, and she fought to free her arms from the sheet. "Can't...breathe," she said.

"JoJo, sweetheart, please wake up." He reached out, daring to touch her in her sleep, moving the hair back from her forehead. "JoJo, it's Max. I'll help you. But you have to wake up."

Tears drenched her face. She looked terrified and so small against the big bed. Unable to stand her tears and sobs a moment longer, Max gathered her into his arms and held her close. If she had struggled, he would have quickly let go. He didn't want his arms to feel like constraints. He worked the sheets loose, allowing her legs and arms free movement. "Breathe," he whispered. "You can breathe now."

JoJo drew in a shuddering breath, and when she let it out, it was as if she released the tension with it. She turned her cheek into his chest and wrapped her arm around his middle. For a long time, he sat on the edge of her bed holding her. His heart hurt for her.

Whatever she had endured had been indelibly etched into her memories. As her struggles ceased, her breathing smoothed and her sobs subsided.

"You're going to be okay, JoJo," he said. "I'm going to make sure you're taken care of." He smiled down at her even though her eyes were closed. "After all, you're my fiancée. You promised to marry me."

An image of her sitting in the ER on the hospital bed filled his memories. She had been smiling, enjoying his discomfort. He'd do it all again just to see her smile. Her eyes lit up when she did. The entire room lit up when JoJo smiled. She needed more reasons to be happy. He hoped that somewhere along the way he could make her smile again. In the meantime, he was just happy he could hold her through her nightmare. As her breathing deepened, he attempted to slide from under her and return to his room, but as he untangled her arm from around his waist, she whimpered.

"It's okay," he said. And brushed her hair back from her forehead. "You're going to be all right." Again, he tried to slip out from under her.

Her hand captured his.

"Please," she said, and her eyes fluttered open. "Don't go. I don't want the dreams to return."

"Try to think of something else. Like kittens, and puppies."

"And babies," she whispered.

"And babies," he agreed. He could imagine a baby

of JoJo's. She'd have dark eyes and jet-black hair just like her mama, and she'd be as beautiful as her mama.

Since she didn't want him to leave, he slid down until he was lying next to her with her body pulled up against his. His groin tightened, and his pulse increased pace as her leg slid over his and her breasts pressed into his chest.

He swallowed a groan. Lying next to her made him only want to hold her longer and closer, preferably naked. But she didn't need that now. She needed him to focus on providing comfort not slaking desire.

His body tense, he tried to relax and go to sleep. It was a long time coming before he finally drifted into a disturbed sleep.

He remained half-awake for a while, afraid his body would react to hers, and he would touch her and take advantage of her without being fully conscious of it. And if she had been assaulted, attempting to make love to her would only frighten her.

So, he lay in a half-sleep, half-awake state loving the feel of her next to him and thinking that it was too bad they weren't really engaged.

JoJo SLEPT the deepest sleep she'd had since she'd woken up in the hospital in Ramstein, Germany. From the moment Max had gathered her into his arms and lay down beside her on the bed, she'd relaxed. She felt safe in his arms.

She blinked her eyes open to the gray light of dawn, as she nestled snugly in the crook of Max's arm. Her cheek rested against his bare chest. She listened to the steady beat of his heart, reassuring in its evenness. Her hand rested on the solidness of his abdomen, his warmth seeping into her.

JoJo could've closed her eyes and gone back to sleep. Instead she lay there, taking in everything about Max, from his woodsy scent, to the hard planes of his muscles. He'd held her without any hint of sexual intent. Had he made a move on her, she probably would've backed away. Now, she lay with her cheek resting on his naked chest, wondering how it would feel to lie naked against his entire body.

Her pulse quickened at the thought, and heat spread from her core outward. What would it feel like to make love with him? Would he be gentle? Would she be receptive? Or would she freeze in the flashbacks of her rape?

His breathing was deep and steady. His eyes closed and his body relaxed. While he slept, light crept into the room. From where she lay, she studied his skin, his muscles and the way his chest rose and fell with each breath. As if of its own accord, her hand moved across his belly and lower.

His muscles twitched beneath her hand.

JoJo froze.

His breathing remained steady, indicating he was still asleep. Unable to resist, she slid her hand even lower. When she reached the elastic band of his boxer shorts, his hand came up and grabbed hers.

"Hey, darling. I don't want you to start something you can't finish."

"What if I want to finish it?" she whispered.

He chuckled and released her hand. "Knock yourself out."

Taking a deep breath, she slid her hand beneath the elastic band and immediately encountered the velvety smooth head of his erection. Her breath lodged in her throat. Caught between the excitement of desire and fear, she hesitated.

"Don't do it if it scares you," Max said.

"You confronted your fears and came out stronger," she reminded him.

"Fear of heights is a lot different than whatever's got you knotted up." He smoothed a hand over her hair. "Look, JoJo, we barely know each other, but I give you my word I would never hurt you."

JoJo nodded. "I believe you." And she did.

"That being said, you need to tell me what you want from me."

She swallowed hard at the lump in her throat. "I don't know what I want."

He slid his hand down her arm. "Sweetheart, I could take you to the very edge and leave you satisfied without ever penetrating you."

JoJo shivered at the velvety silkiness of his tone. His talk about sex made the heat at her core flame. "What about you?" she asked. "What if I don't want to…"

He chuckled. "I could be more than satisfied just to see you come apart."

A shiver of desire rippled through her.

His hand swept up her arm and back down. "I can go as slow or as fast as you want."

She stilled, her heart beating hard against her chest. "What if I want you to stop?"

He drew in a deep breath and let it out slowly. "Then I'll stop. *You'll* be in control. And *only* you."

With him touching her body, she doubted that she would be in much control.

"Or we could just lie here and enjoy each other's company." His arm tightened slightly around her, and then loosened.

He'd placed no demands on her or her body. Which made touching him even more tempting. "Go slowly," she whispered, and then held her breath wondering if he'd heard her.

Several seconds passed before he asked, "Are you sure?"

She nodded, her cheek rubbing against his chest as she did. Then she tilted her head up to look into his eyes as he looked down at her, and she spoke a little louder. "Go slowly."

Max shifted to where he was lying on his side

facing her. He cupped her cheek in his hand and leaned forward to press his lips to hers. His hands slipped from her shoulder down her arm and rested on the swell of her hip. "If you feel at all uncomfortable, tell me and I'll stop."

JoJo nodded, staring straight into his eyes. She didn't tell him that she had already felt uncomfortable, but it was a different kind of uncomfortable. One that was in anticipation of what titillating things he might do to her.

Still lying on his side, he inched his way downward on the bed, trailing kisses across her collarbone and down to claim the tip of one nipple beneath the fabric of her pajama top.

Needing to feel his lips on her skin, JoJo pulled the hem of her top up, exposing her breasts. He flicked a nipple before capturing it between his teeth and rolling it gently.

JoJo's back arched, urging him to take more.

He sucked the nipple into his mouth and pulled hard.

JoJo's breath caught and held as he flicked and licked the nipple into a tight little bud. JoJo's breathing grew ragged, and her body tensed. Not because she was afraid, but because she wanted more.

He abandoned that breast and moved to the other. He treated that breast to the same licking, nipping, and tickling.

JoJo reached for his head and wove her fingers

into his hair, holding him closer. If she wanted, she could've pushed him away, but she didn't. How could she, when what he was doing to her made her entire body light on fire and crave more from him?

He smoothed his hand down to her waist and back up over her hip, cupping her buttocks as his mouth moved lower, skimming across her ribs inch by inch as he traveled down her body to the juncture of her thighs.

JoJo rolled onto her back, drawing in shallow, rapid breaths. The closer he got to her core, the more tense she grew. Her fingers in his hair tightened, and he slowed to a stop.

He looked up. "Do you want me to stop here?"

"Yes... No."

He chuckled, his breath warm against her belly. "I don't have to go any farther."

"But I want..." She bit down hard on her bottom lip. She wanted him but she was afraid. "Go slower," she said.

"I can do that." He pressed a kiss between her belly button and the tuft of hair over her sex.

JoJo ran her tongue across her suddenly dry lips.

His mouth moved just slightly lower, and he pressed a kiss to her. He continued kissing her until he reached the mound of hair. He laid his hand lightly over it. "Tell me when to stop, and I will."

"Don't...stop."

With his thumbs, he parted her folds and leaned

in to flick her there with his tongue. She drew in a sharp breath and held it until he flicked again. The air left her lungs in a whoosh. He licked her again, and a moan rose up her throat and escaped her lips.

What he was doing was magic. She still couldn't remember the actual rape, but it couldn't have been anything like this. And he hadn't touched her there. He'd promised not to penetrate her, and she believed he'd keep to his promise. Knowing in her heart that this was as far as he would go, she relaxed as much as she could and let her body rejoice in what he was doing. Slowly and steadily, he touched her there, his tongue sending wicked electrical currents reverberating throughout her body. He increased the speed and swirled his tongue.

JoJo raised her hips off the mattress wanting somehow to get closer to him. What had started as a want had built to a need. As he flicked and swirled, her body tensed. The sensations building and growing until that one last flick that sent her over the edge.

She cried out his name. "Max." Her hands convulsed in his hair. Her body pulsed with her release. She clung to those sensations for as long as they lasted, reveling in the feeling of pure satisfaction. When the last tingle subsided, she fell back against the bed.

He chuckled and climbed up her body to lean over her, the length of his cock resting against her inner thigh. When he leaned down to kiss her, his chest pressed against hers.

JoJo wasn't sure if it was the weight of him or the pressure against her lungs, but suddenly she felt trapped and she pushed against his chest.

He immediately backed off and dropped down beside her. "Sorry," he said. "I didn't mean to scare you."

She shook her head, drawing in deep breaths. "No, no that's okay," she said. "I just couldn't breathe." She rolled over onto her side and faced him, laying her hand on his chest. "Do you mind if I touch you?"

He smiled. "Are you kidding me? Of course not."

She ran her fingers over his chest stopping at a scar. "How did you get this?"

"Shrapnel wound."

She leaned forward and pressed her lips to it. Then, with her fingers, she continued her perusal to a scar lower down on his torso. "And this one?"

He smiled. "Got that one when I ran into a barbed wire fence on my bicycle when I was nine years old." He shrugged. "I didn't want to tell my mother about it because I was somewhere I wasn't supposed to be. When she found out, she was mad, but not because I'd been there, but because I'd lied to her. Either way, I got grounded."

She kissed that scar too and moved her fingers even lower. She was now down below his belly button at the next scar. "And this?"

It was a long scar, four inches or more.

"That one was from my fall." It was a brighter pink than the other scars, as if it were a newer one.

She scooted down the bed and pressed her lips to that one. "I'm sorry this happened to you."

"Not as sorry as I was while I was falling two hundred and fifty feet to the ground."

"That had to have been terrifying."

His lips twisted. "The only thought I remember as I fell was that I knew it was going to hurt. They were quick to get a rescue team out there and get me to a trauma center. If they hadn't reacted so quickly, I probably would've been dead."

"I, for one, am glad you lived."

He cupped her cheek. "Me, too. Although, there was a time that I wasn't so glad."

She nodded. "I know how you feel." Her hand slipped lower to the elastic of his boxer shorts.

"You don't have to do this," he said.

"I know. Which makes me want to even more." She slid her hand inside his shorts and cupped him, rolling his balls between her fingers. Then she wrapped her hand around him and slid to the tip of his cock and back down.

She wanted him. JoJo swallowed hard. She wanted him inside her, but it had to be on her terms. She grabbed the waistband of his shorts and dragged them over his hips.

He lifted his bottom off the mattress, allowing her

to take them all the way down to his ankles. His cock jetted out, hard, long and thick.

The combination of excitement and fear swelled in her chest. Once he lay naked in the bed, she straddled his hips. "I don't suppose you have protection?"

He shook his head. "Not on me. But I do have it in my room."

She rolled over onto the bed.

"Are you sure that's what you want?" he asked before moving.

She nodded.

Max was off the bed in a flash, racing through the connecting door and back in less than thirty seconds.

He laughed and held up the packet. Then he dropped onto the bed beside her, pulled her into his arms and kissed her.

She pushed him onto his back, took the packet from his fingers, ripped it open and rolled it down over his cock. JoJo straddled him, and then lowered herself. She didn't want too much time to think. She wanted to act before she lost her nerve.

She dropped down until the tip of his cock nudged her entrance. Her breath hitched in her throat, and her hands grew clammy. She took a deep breath and lowered herself onto him, taking him into herself slowly, her channel adjusting to his girth.

She tried not to think about what had happened to her. She should be thankful that part of her memory had been erased. This time, she was in control. She made the decisions. Nothing was forced on her. As he filled her to full, she let out a low moan. It felt good…really good. She rocked up on her knees, letting him slide back out until his tip hovered at her entrance. She sank back down and settled into a smooth rhythm. Raising and lowering.

He wrapped his hands around her buttocks, holding her without adding pressure. He let her ride him.

JoJo could feel his body tense beneath her. His grip tightened on her ass. He gently guided her pace, thrusting deep and steadily. His grip tightened, and he thrust one more time, holding her down on top of him. She felt that familiar tingling at her center spreading outward as she climaxed again with his cock throbbing inside her. For a long moment, she rested her hands on his chest, letting the sensations wash over her. Then she collapsed on top of him.

The sun streamed through the window, creating a glow around them.

Max rolled her onto her side and pulled her close. She nestled her head in the crook of his arm. She rested her hand on his chest and draped one of her calves over his leg.

"Do you still want to know what happened to me?" she asked.

His hand on her arm stopped moving. "Yes, I do."

She didn't look up into his eyes. She studied her hand on his chest. "I don't know exactly what happened," she said, "because my memories of the incident have been blocked in my brain. Some kind of situational amnesia, but from what the EMT and the doctors told me when I came to, I'd been raped, beaten, and buried alive."

He tensed.

JoJo looked up at him. "I hope you're not mad at me."

"Sweet Jesus, JoJo!" he exclaimed. "You should've told me before—"

"Before we had sex?"

He shook his head. "Before we made love."

"Why?" she asked. "Because you wouldn't have?"

He shook his head again. "I still would have, but I would've been even more gentle."

She smiled up at him. "I'm safe," she said. "No STD's. I had them test me."

He pulled her into his arms and rested his chin on her head. "I'm so sorry this happened to you. Did they catch the bastard who did it?"

She shook her head. "No. He's still out there, possibly raping other women. I wouldn't be alive today if it hadn't been for a dog digging me out and some Afghan women finding me."

"I can't even comprehend how somebody could do that to a person?" Max said. "It really makes you lose faith in the human race."

JoJo nodded. "But I have to tell myself there aren't that many people who would do such a thing. And then

I think about the women who found me and sought help. And then the medic who helped me into the helicopter. The pilots who flew me to the air staging unit, and then the medical staff who were with me all the way to Ramstein. There are far more good people in this world than bad. But since he's still out there, I can't feel safe. And the thought of him doing something similar to another woman just eats at me. I wish I could pull the memory out of my brain so that I could identify him and get him locked up for life." She looked away from his gaze. "I thought what he did had ruined me for life, that having sex with anybody would be too traumatic."

"You're still you," Max said tucking a stray hair back behind her ear. "You're worthy of love. Don't let one man's crime define you."

"I was so afraid that people would look at me differently. That they'd treat me as if I'd brought it on myself." She swallowed hard. "That I deserved to be raped."

Max cursed. "No woman deserves to be raped or beaten or buried alive. No woman or man deserves such a fate. Any person who would think that you brought it on yourself, doesn't deserve your time of day."

"I should've told you before we made love," she said. "You should've understood what you were getting into. But I was kind of following your advice."

He chuckled. "And what advice was that?"

"I feared that I'd never be able to enjoy sex again." She met his gaze. "I feared that I'd be afraid of a man's touch. So, I followed your advice and confronted my fears."

Max smoothed a thumb across her cheek. "And you came out stronger for it."

She nodded.

"And are you still afraid of making love?" he asked.

"Yes and no."

He smiled. "As long as you're on top you're okay, right?"

She nodded. "Does that bother you?"

"Far from it. You're doing all the work, and you're in control, which I'm fully okay with."

She basked in his warm gaze and acceptance, not ready to leave the security of his arms. But life went on, and they had a job to do. "I guess we should be thinking about getting up. It's daylight outside. I'm usually in the barn by now."

He held her close and snuggled with her. "I wonder if anybody would notice us missing if we just didn't show up?"

JoJo laughed. "RJ would come looking for me. Besides, I wouldn't leave her to handle all this on her own. It's sure to be an incredibly busy day."

He kissed her forehead, the tip of her nose, and then finally her lips. When he came up, he stared down into her eyes. "Thank you for telling me. I know it took a lot for you to open up."

"It did." Her lips pressed into a thin line. "I wish that regaining my memories would be as easy."

"Maybe about the time you quit trying to recall what happened, those memories will return."

She smiled. "That's what Emily says."

His brow wrinkled. "Emily is…?"

"A friend of Gunny and RJ's. She'll be out later to help, and I think she's going to put me through some hypnosis to see if I can jog those memories loose."

"Are you sure you want to relive those? Your mind may know that it's better to keep them hidden. The trauma of reliving it could cause damage."

She shook her head. "I'd rather know who did this and live with the consequences of regaining my memories than live in fear until the man is caught."

"I can understand," he said. He rolled out of the bed and held his hand out.

She placed her hand in his, and he helped her to her feet.

He waggled his brows. "Think anybody would notice if we crossed the hall naked and get into the shower together?"

JoJo laughed. "My luck, Gunny would be standing out in the hallway to see us." She gathered her bathrobe off the floor where it had slipped off the bed. While she was at it, she lifted his boxer shorts off the floor and handed them to him. "But we could go across the hall semi-dressed."

He slipped on his shorts, she slipped on her robe and they grabbed clothes. Max ducked into his room for a second, and then they hustled across the hall. In the bathroom, they showered together, which led to another round of lovemaking with full-on sex with the condom Max had secured from his room.

JoJo could get used to Max running his hands all over her body. It didn't make her feel strange, awkward or anything but sexy and desirable. And the fact that he still wanted to hold her after she'd told him she'd been raped, said a lot about his character and eased her mind. Max gave her hope for the future.

CHAPTER 13

AFTER MAKING LOVE WITH JoJo, Max was conflicted. On the one hand, he felt very blessed that she'd let him touch her and make love to her. On the other hand, he felt cursed he hadn't known before. He probably wouldn't have made love to her, afraid that it would frighten her and further damage her psyche. But JoJo seemed a little more relaxed after their romp in the bed and the shower. She even smiled several times. He patted her dry and wrapped her in the big towel, kissing her forehead again. "Don't be afraid to tell me how you feel," he said. "What you went through is a lot harder than falling from a two hundred and fifty foot cliff."

She cocked an eyebrow. "I didn't break every bone in my body, and I'm not limping."

Max shook his head. "You know what I mean."

"I know I'll never get over it. But I will get past it,"

she said. "And who knows? Maybe the hypnosis will help me figure out who the guy was. Plus, I've asked RJ to contact Hank and see if his computer guy can find out what's going on with the investigation. Surely, they've gotten some kind of lead by now."

Once more he pulled her gently into his arms and kissed her.

She wrapped her arms around his neck and drew him closer, deepening the kiss. She stared up at him through narrowed eyes. "Don't treat me as if I am going to break. I'm stronger than that."

He touched the back of his head with a wink. "Don't I know it." His smile faded, "And now, I know why you flipped me and what freaked you out when Roy grabbed you." He took her hand and raised it to his lips. "Come on, let's get this weekend over with."

She grinned up at him. "You feel that way, too?"

He nodded. "I'm not much into political candidates. They always seem kind of fake to me."

"Ditto," she said,

Still holding hands, they walked out of the bathroom to find RJ standing in the hallway.

RJ's brows rose.

Before her friend could open her mouth, JoJo raised a finger. "Don't say a word."

RJ performed an about face and marched the other direction and down the stairs, calling out over her shoulder, "I want all the details later."

JoJo groaned.

"You could always tell her that you were showing me where the towels were."

JoJo raised her hand with his connected to hers. "And how do I explain us holding hands coming out of the bathroom? You don't have to hold hands to get a towel out."

"The beauty of it is, you don't have to explain yourself to anyone," Max said.

JoJo grinned. "You're right. I'm a grown woman."

They descended the stairs, still holding hands, but when they got to the bottom, JoJo pulled hers free. He glanced her way.

She gave him a crooked smile. "The fewer questions asked the better."

He nodded. "Good thinking."

They joined Jake, Cage, Gunny and RJ in the dining room. A platter of eggs, a stack of pancakes and a plate full of bacon were set out on the table along with a carafe of coffee.

Max's stomach rumbled.

RJ was on her way back to the kitchen. "Don't wait on me. Dig in while it's hot. And a big shoutout to Gunny and Jake for cooking breakfast this morning."

Everyone took a seat at the table, and RJ joined them carrying a pitcher of orange juice.

Max looked around the dining room. All of the other tables were empty. "Did Stover and Curry go out for breakfast?"

RJ shook her head. "No, they decided to have breakfast here earlier than planned. They said they had some things to do in town and at the casino, so they wanted to get an early start."

Max sat on one side of JoJo.

RJ sat on the other. She leaned close to JoJo and whispered.

Max strained to hear what she said but couldn't quite catch her words.

JoJo turned to RJ. "He knows."

JoJo looked across the table at Max and said quietly, "I told him."

RJ shot a glance toward Max as well.

He dipped his head once in acknowledgement.

Jake and Gunny were in deep conversation and unaware of what was being spoken between RJ, JoJo and Max.

"Did she tell you that I contacted Hank?" RJ asked.

Again, Max dipped his head.

"He's got his guy Swede working on it. From what I understand about Swede, if there's anything in the system about the investigation, he'll find it."

"Good," Max said.

RJ clapped her hands together. "So, what's on the agenda today?"

Gunny glanced up from his conversation with Jake and Cage. "The campaign team will arrive sometime after noon. They'll have a conference until about five and eat dinner at six. After that, I suggested an icebreaker of a hayride, and after that making s'mores by the fire pit."

"I'll hitch the tractor to the wagon," JoJo said. "We could use some help piling hay onto the wagon."

"I could help with that," Max said.

"As can we," Jake said.

Cage raised his hand in affirmation.

"I'll make sure the firepit is stocked up with wood to burn and clean up the sticks we'll use to roast marshmallows," Gunny said.

"And I'll tend to some of the horses' hooves and grooming," RJ said. "Then I've got some things I need to do inside the house to make sure all the bedrooms are ready, and the laundry is all caught up."

"I'll take care of the dishes," JoJo said.

"And so will I," Max offered.

While everyone left the lodge, JoJo and Max went to the kitchen with a tray of dishes. It seemed like every time JoJo turned around, she bumped into Max, which wasn't a hardship by any stretch of the imagination. In fact, she might've been doing it on purpose.

Eventually, Max caught on, grabbed her around the waist, pulled her up against him and nuzzled her ear.

"I'd almost bet that in the bodyguard handbook, bodyguards aren't supposed to be kissing on the bodies they're guarding." JoJo laughed. "Not that I'm complaining."

"Say the word, and I'll stop," he said.

She turned in his arms and poked his chest. "Don't stop. I kind of like that you bother me."

"Good, because you bother me, too, in a whole different way." He pulled her close and let her feel the hard ridge of his cock pressing against his jeans into her belly.

After finishing the dishes, the two went out into the barn. Max performed as ground guide while JoJo backed the tractor into the hitch for the trailer. Once they had that secured, they went to work loading the trailer with bales of hay. Jake and Cage helped.

They loaded one layer of hay and a second one near the front. Guests would sit on the bales of hay as JoJo drove the tractor around the pasture. When the wagon was ready, they all joined Gunny around the firepit. He had unstacked the ring of stones and was one by one restacking them neatly. Jake bent to help him, getting it done quickly, while Cage, Max and JoJo gathered some of the split logs from the stack against the barn.

Stover and Curry remained gone all morning, giving the Lost Valley Ranch crew plenty of time to make sure everything was in place before the campaign staff arrived and Curry and Stover returned.

Just before noon, a small black SUV arrived. They'd all just settled on the porch with glasses of iced tea and lemonade. A woman got out of the SUV.

She was a little bit taller than JoJo and as blond as JoJo was dark haired. She smiled and waved at RJ and JoJo. They stepped down off the porch and went to hug the woman. As they climbed the stairs, RJ smiled at the group on the porch.

"Jake, Cage, Max, this is Emily, a friend of ours. In fact, she used to live here for a while. Now, she has her own practice down in Colorado Springs, working at the veterans hospital." RJ turned to Cage. "Emily, this is Cage Weaver."

Cage shook hands with Emily. "Nice to meet you, ma'am."

Emily laughed. "Please don't call me ma'am. Makes me feel old."

"Yes, ma'am." Cage grimaced. "Yes, Emily."

Emily laughed and shook her head. "Never mind."

RJ waved toward Max. "Emily, this is Max."

Max shook Emily's hand. "Nice to meet you, Emily."

"Pleasure's mine," she said.

"And this is Jake, the man I've been telling you about."

Emily grinned and shook his hand. "I'm so glad to meet you, Jake. Every time I talk to RJ, all she has to say is Jake this and Jake that. Glad to finally meet the man behind the name. I can't tell you how much happier RJ seems to be."

RJ laughed. "Who would've thought I'd ever find someone to love?"

Emily lifted her chin. "I knew you'd find some-body someday. I'm glad it was sooner rather than later."

"These three gentlemen are a part of that group I was telling you about," RJ continued. "The Brother-hood Protectors. They're the ones who are reno-vating the basement of the lodge to use as their headquarters here in Colorado. They're based out of Montana with a branch office here in Colorado."

Emily grinned. "I can't wait to see what they've done with that old dusty basement."

"If you want to come with me," Jake said. "I'll show you."

Emily turned to JoJo. "JoJo?"

"Our session can wait," JoJo said. "Go see the basement. They've done an amazing transformation down there."

"Why don't we all go down there?" Gunny said. "It's been a couple days since I've been to check out the work that's been done."

"You guys go ahead," JoJo said. "I'm going to gather up the glasses and get them into the dishwasher."

Max hung back.

JoJo smiled. "I'll be all right. I'm just going to the kitchen, and then I'll join you."

"I can wait," Max said.

"No, really. I need to make a trip to the bathroom as well. Then I'll join you downstairs."

Max hesitated.

"Seriously," JoJo said, "I'll be fine."

He reluctantly turned away and followed the group down to the basement. The workers had been there the day before finishing up some trim work. They were waiting to open the facility until some pieces of equipment were delivered. By the next week, they anticipated being fully up and running.

Emily exclaimed her approval of the transformation.

After several minutes, JoJo still hadn't shown up. Max headed up the stairs. He didn't like it when she was out of his sight. Not that he thought anything would happen while they were in the lodge, but she could never be too careful.

He climbed the stairs and entered the kitchen. JoJo wasn't there. Max went to the downstairs bathroom and knocked on the door. Nobody answered. He pushed open the door. She wasn't in the bathroom. He climbed the stairs to her room and knocked on the door there. Again, she wasn't in her room, and she wasn't in the bathroom across the hall.

Starting to get worried, he went back out on to the porch to see if maybe she had forgotten some items of dishes that she had wanted to put in the dishwasher.

JoJo was nowhere to be seen.

His heart started pounding harder, and his pulse raced. Another vehicle was parked beside Emily's that hadn't been there when they'd gone into the basement. It was the one Stover and Curry had used, and they too were nowhere to be seen in the places Max had just checked.

Knowing JoJo couldn't stay away from the barn for long, Max headed there next, praying she was there and that he found her alone.

CHAPTER 14

JoJo had had every intention of joining the others in the basement. As she had come out of the kitchen, she'd remembered that she'd left her cellphone in the barn. She hurried out to go find it. While she was there, she could perform one last check to make sure everything was in place for that evening's activities.

She found her cellphone where she'd left it in the tack room on the desk. After tucking it into her back pocket, she turned to leave, only to find somebody standing in the doorway blocking her exit from the tack room.

"Ah, Ms. Ramirez," Stover said. "I'm glad I caught you out here."

JoJo stiffened and forced a smile to her face. "Mr. Stover, what can I do for you?"

His eyebrows rose. "I just wanted to make sure everything was in place for this evening's events."

JoJo didn't like that he was blocking her way out of the tack room. She looked over his shoulder to see his aide Curry lurking in the shadows in the barn. Her pulse quickened. Maybe she was being overly sensitive, but she felt trapped. Cornered like a mouse in a cage. "Everything's ready, Mr. Stover. Now, if you'll excuse me, I need to get back to the lodge."

"If everything's ready, what's your hurry?" He didn't move out of the doorway. His body completely blocked her escape.

"RJ and Gunny are expecting me at the lodge," she explained. "Then we're going over to the Watering Hole to set up for the lunch crowd."

"Well, then by all means, don't let me keep you." He turned sideways in the threshold, leaving barely enough room for anybody to get by.

It was enough for JoJo. She darted between Stover and the doorframe. She brushed against Stover as she squeezed passed him, only to come face to face with Curry. "Do you need something, Mr. Curry?" she asked, her tone a little abrupt.

His eyes narrowed. "There's something very familiar about you," he said. "Are you sure we didn't serve together?"

"I don't know," she said, starting to get a little anxious. She needed to get outside into the fresh air with plenty of room to move. "There's a lot of people in the Army. We may have served together somewhere. Now, please, excuse me. I need to be somewhere." Anywhere besides there, with these two men.

His eyes narrowed even more, but he stepped aside.

JoJo made a dash for the barn door. She didn't slow down until she was out in the glaring sunlight. Temporarily blinded, she ran into a wall. Strong arms wrapped around her.

"Hey there, beautiful," his voice sounded in her ear, his voice absolutely identifiable.

Immediately, JoJo relaxed against Max.

"You okay?" he asked.

She nodded. "I'm fine."

"Good, because I told Gunny we'd get started opening up the Watering Hole."

"I'm ready, let's go." She took his hand and practically dragged him over to the bar.

"Are you sure you're okay?" he asked.

"I'm fine. Just a little creeped out by Stover and Curry," she said as she unlocked the back door of the bar. "I ran into them in the barn."

"That must be whose car was sitting next to Emily's. Were they bothering you?" he asked.

"Only because I didn't expect to turn around and see them in the barn."

Max turned before he entered the Watering Hole and stared back at the barn. JoJo's gaze followed his. Stover and Curry were standing outside the barn door talking.

"I don't know what it is about those two," he said. "I just don't trust them."

JoJo laughed. "Must be that they're politicians."

"No, I don't think it's that," he said, his gaze still on the barn and the two men. "They weren't always politicians. They served in the military, which usually I can relate with."

"It doesn't matter. Let's get this lunch crowd fed and watered and get ready for the evening's fun."

While JoJo cranked up the grill, Max went through the dining room, unlocked the door and set the chairs on the floor. As he finished, the first patrons walked through the entrance.

For the next couple of hours JoJo, Max, RJ, Gunny, Cage and Jake were busy filling orders for drinks and food. Once the lunch crowd was gone, they had to hurry to clean up the bar and be ready for when the campaign staff would show up.

Stover's team arrived shortly after the Lost Valley Ranch crew had just finished cleaning the bar.

The rest of the evening was a blur of activity, keeping the guests fed and entertained. After their dinner, JoJo drove the tractor around the pasture with the guests onboard, and Max rode in the wagon with the guests. The s'mores around the firepit were a big hit. By the time hot cocoa had been consumed and everybody was shown to their rooms, JoJo was tired.

Emily found her in the kitchen cleaning up after

the hot cocoa bar. "We never did get around to our hypnosis session," she said.

"Maybe there will be time in the morning," JoJo said. "I'm too tired to do this tonight."

"Actually, now might be a good time to do this. How about you come to RJ's room, and we'll give it a shot. If it doesn't work tonight, then we'll try again in the morning."

JoJo nodded. Even though she was tired, she was ready to get the memory recollection done. JoJo rinsed the last dish, put it in the dishwasher and started it. She wiped her hands and followed Emily up the stairs to her room.

RJ's room had an old-fashioned white iron bed with a quilted top. Near the window were two wing backed chairs in a floral print. JoJo sat in one, and Emily sat in the other. Emily kept her voice in a low monotone, unlike her usual melodious tones. She spoke barely above a whisper, easing JoJo into a trance.

As she was listening, JoJo thought this was all a bunch of baloney but, if it helped, the more power to her. She let herself relax and grow calm and just listen to the smooth cadence of Emily's voice. She must have fallen asleep because she found herself in her nightmare again where a man was holding her down, hitting her.

"Look at his face," a voice said into her dream.

JoJo wanted to keep her eyes squeezed shut.

"Open your eyes and look at his face," the disembodied voice said.

JoJo forced her eyes open. She was lying in the dirt, and someone was hovering over her.

"Look at his eyes. What color are his eyes?"

She stared up at the man. It was too dark outside to determine exactly the color of his eyes. Starlight glinted off of them. "They're a light color," JoJo said as the man punched her in the face. She cried out in pain.

"His hair. What color is his hair?" the voice insisted.

The man's hair wasn't really dark or really light. In the veil of night, she couldn't tell the exact color.

"Look for tattoos," the voice urged.

JoJo took in his face, his neck, his arms. "None," she whispered.

"What is he wearing?" the voice asked.

"Uniform," she said.

"Can you see his name tag or his rank?"

She tried to focus on the front of his shirt. The man above her hit her in the face and hit her again. Pain shot through her. He hit her again and again, until she was weeping.

"It's okay, JoJo. Wake up. It's okay, JoJo. Wake up, JoJo," the voice said.

She didn't want to open her eyes. She didn't want to see who it was that was hitting her.

"Open your eyes, JoJo. It's okay. Wake up, it's just a dream."

She opened her eyes to find herself looking across into Emily's face.

Emily reached out and touched her knee. "It's okay, JoJo. You're safe. You're with me."

"He was hitting me."

"I'm so sorry." Emily squeezed her knee. "Had you ever had him hitting you in your nightmares before?"

"Yes, but this time, I saw his hands swinging at me."

"And did you see his face?"

JoJo closed her eyes for a moment trying to recall. "It was dark."

"His face was dark?"

"No, it was dark outside. I couldn't see his features, but in the starlight, the night sky glinted on his eyes. They were a light color."

"Good," Emily said. "What about his hair?"

"It was short. It wasn't really dark, and it wasn't really light. Again, it was dark outside. Couldn't really tell what color it was." A tear slipped from her eye and ran down her cheek. "He just kept hitting me."

Emily took her hand and squeezed it. "We don't have to do this."

JoJo shook her head. "Yes, we do. The more I remember, the better chance I have of identifying him."

Emily smiled. "Hey, well, you're remembering *some* things."

"Maybe we should keep going," JoJo said.

Emily shook her head. "No, that's enough for tonight. We don't want to push too hard and make you shut down again."

JoJo wanted to keep going, to learn who the man was who'd hurt her. But Emily was right. She couldn't keep pushing if it meant she'd go back to no memories at all.

"Thank you, Emily," JoJo said. "I feel like I'm one step closer to remembering."

"Keep up the hope, but don't expect it to happen all at once." Emily patted her knee. "You'd better get some sleep. Tomorrow's going to be an extra busy day."

"You're right. It's going to be a long day." JoJo rose from her chair. "I hope you get some rest."

Emily rose, walked with her to the door and gave her a big hug before she opened the door and let her out.

"Thank you, Emily," JoJo said again.

"We'll try again tomorrow, if you're up to it."

JoJo walked through the door and nearly ran into Max who was leaning against the wall. "Geez, you scared me."

He straightened. "Sorry, I just wanted to make sure you were okay."

"I'm fine. I was just having a session with Emily."

"Did she help you remember anything?"

JoJo took in a deep breath and blew it out slowly. "I don't know. Maybe. This hypnosis thing is kind of scary and, at the same time, it just might be the key to accessing those memories I can't reach when I'm awake. It was like I was in a dream. Only this time, I could remember bits and pieces."

He walked with her down the hall to her bedroom. When she opened the door he said, "Let me look first."

"Do you really think there would be a problem in my bedroom here in the lodge?"

"Did you ever think that somebody would sabotage your apartment and blow it up with a gas leak?"

She shook her head. "It's all yours."

It took him two seconds to look through the room, and he was back out. "It's all clear. If you need me, you'll know where I'll be," he said. "Lock your door behind me."

JoJo entered her room and closed the door.

"I didn't hear your lock click," Max said from the other side of the door.

JoJo laughed and twisted the lock. "Satisfied?"

He chuckled. "I am now."

She could hear his footsteps moving down the hall, and his door opening and closing. She ran to the connecting door, unlocked it and flung it open. "Did you lock your door?"

He smiled. "I sure did."

She leaned against the door frame. "I'm going to get a shower. Care to join me?"

His brow furrowed. "Are you ready?"

"Ready for what?"

"To pick up where we left off."

"I think so."

He shook his head. "Go get your shower, JoJo."

She frowned. Feeling thoroughly dismissed and a little angry, she turned away, closed the door, gathered her things and went across the hall to the bathroom. She'd barely closed the door when a knock sounded on it. JoJo smiled and opened the door, "I thought you—"

She expected to see Max standing there. Instead, she found Curry. She had always wondered what it meant by having your blood run cold. Up until that point, she hadn't known what it meant. Now, she did.

Curry's eyes narrowed. "Sorry, didn't know the place was occupied."

"JoJo," Max called out.

She looked around Curry to see Max headed her way. Her pulse was pounding. Something about Curry's dark eyes seemed somehow familiar.

"Mr. Curry, have we met before?" she asked.

His brow dipped. "I'm sure I would remember if we had," he said. "I'll leave you to the bathroom." He turned and walked down the corridor to the other end.

Max hurried toward her, carrying his shaving kit.

"I changed my mind," he said, and entered the bathroom and closed the door behind them. Then he pulled her into his arms. "I don't know what it is about that guy, but he gives me the creeps. Trust me, it takes a lot to give me the creeps."

JoJo rested her cheek against his chest. "I feel the same way. I don't know what it is about him either."

"We don't have to shower together," he said. "But I'll stay in here with you while you shower just to make sure you're safe. That is, if you want me to."

She lifted the hem of his shirt and pulled it up over his head. "I want you to stay." While she helped him out of his clothes, he helped her out of hers, and soon they were standing together beneath the spray.

"Did you bring—"

He reached outside the shower for his shaving kit and produced a condom. "At this rate, I'm going to need to get a new supply."

She smiled. "Yes, you will."

He sheathed himself then lifted her by the backs of her thighs, pressing her against the cold tiles of the shower wall. "Tell me if I do anything that scares you."

"I will." She captured his face between her palms and kissed him.

After they sated themselves in the shower, they dried each other off, dressed and crossed the hall into her bedroom.

"Do you want me to stay?" he asked.

She took his hand and led him to the bed. "Yes, I do. When you were with me last night, I didn't have dreams."

"But isn't that the idea of having dreams, so that you can remember what happened?"

"I'll leave that to Emily and hypnotism. I'd rather get a good night's sleep. I hadn't had one until you slept with me."

He frowned. "How long has it been?"

"Over six months," she said.

Max picked her up and laid her in the bed then crawled in beside her. He pulled her into his arms.

"I want you to know it's not all about the sex," she said.

He chuckled. "That's my line."

JoJo smiled. "I just want to hold you through the night, and I want you to hold me."

She lay there nestled in his arms and fell into a deep dreamless sleep, thinking how nice it would be if she could do this every night.

If only.

CHAPTER 15

Max woke before JoJo the next morning and crossed
to his room where he dressed. By the time he came
back to check on her, she was up and dressed as well.
"How'd you sleep?" he asked.

"Never better," she said. "Thank you."

He didn't want her thanks. He wanted her healthy
and happy. "We'd better get downstairs and help with
the breakfast to feed all the people that are here."

The day flew by as they kept the campaign staff in
the conference room flush with water and snacks. RJ,
Jake, JoJo and Max managed the lunch crowd at the
bar and set up for the afternoon meet and greet.
Stover had arranged to have a band there.

Cage and Jake were given parking duty to direct
the guests into a field where they could park their
cars. Max worked with JoJo making sure the guests
had drinks. RJ, Gunny and Emily worked the food

with Gunny at the grill, making hot dogs and hamburgers. RJ and Emily kept a table of sides and condiments refreshed.

Stover's campaign team hung banners and patriotic signs throughout the area. Stover was the star of the show, standing at the center of attention as the guests came to meet him. He smiled and shook hands, with Curry standing nearby to help him with any other needs.

After the meet and greet was officially over, a significant portion of the guests adjourned to the Watering Hole to continue the party there. Stover and Curry ended up in the bar as well. Max and JoJo made the drinks, while Emily, RJ and Jake served.

By the time the last person left, Max's leg ached. He could just imagine how Jake felt, being on his prosthetic all day long. Neither one of them complained. It wasn't in their nature. By the time everybody had left, they were all so exhausted.

Emily came by the bar where Max and JoJo were finishing up. "I know it's late and you're tired, but do you want to do another session tonight? Or we could wait until the morning."

JoJo shook her head. "I'm exhausted and tomorrow morning is going to be really busy, getting everybody fed and out the door for the day's team-building activities."

"Then maybe tomorrow night since everybody's

going out to eat, we can do one more hypnosis session before I leave on Sunday."

JoJo nodded. "That would work."

"Is there anything I can do to help in here?" A voice called out behind JoJo and Max. They turned to find Stover standing at the entrance to the kitchen. "I already asked Gunny if he needed help cleaning in the kitchen, but he said he had everything under control."

"We're about done in here," JoJo said.

"What's this about hypnosis?" Stover asked.

Emily smiled. "Nothing. Do you or any of your guests want a hot cocoa bar tonight?" she asked and walked over to where Stover stood. "Why don't you walk me back to the lodge, and let's ask the others."

Cage emerged from the kitchen "I'll go with you." The three left the Watering Hole. Gunny, Jake and RJ emerged from the kitchen.

"Done here?" Gunny asked.

"Done," Max said. They headed out the back door and walked across to the lodge.

Once inside, they found the campaign staff lounging in the great room by the fire, sipping hot cocoa or coffee.

RJ turned to Max and JoJo. "You two go on up. Gunny and I will take care of this."

JoJo shook her head. "You're just as tired as we are. We can stay a little longer and help."

"No." RJ crossed her arms over her chest. "I insist."

JoJo lifted her chin. "Then we'll get up early and start breakfast."

"Deal," RJ said with a smile.

JoJo and Max walked up the stairs.

"Gunny will be down here at four-thirty in the morning to get breakfast started no matter what," JoJo commented.

"I kind of figured that," Max said. "But maybe RJ will sleep in."

She snorted. "Not a chance."

"One more day," Max said, "and then they all leave."

They showered together and lay in bed. Before long, they were making love. Max let JoJo be on top, knowing what it meant to her. Afterward, she fell asleep in his arms and slept the entire night through with no nightmares.

Max had stayed right with her during the day, and he'd vowed to stay with her the next day as well. He liked being with JoJo.

Thankfully, the day had gone by without incident. Nobody had made an attempt on JoJo's life. Being with her had helped. Having so many people around made him nervous. He couldn't watch everybody all the time, so he'd concentrated his efforts and his attention on JoJo.

One more day, and they'd be through the big event. Then it would be back to smaller crowds, making it easier for him to guard her and keep her safe. He figured he'd already broken every rule a bodyguard should live by. Don't get involved with your client. Don't sleep with your client. And don't fall in love with your client. He figured he was well on his way to failing all three of those.

SATURDAY MORNING WAS a repeat of the previous morning. All Lost Valley Ranch hands were on deck to get the campaign staff fed and out the door for the day's activities.

Once they had the guests served, the ranch hands sat down to their meal. They ate quickly and went back to work.

While the campaign staff met in the conference room, RJ, Emily and Jake stayed in the lodge to clean up the dining room and kitchen. Cage, JoJo and Max cleared the tables.

JoJo carried the last tray of dirty dishes into the kitchen and set it on the counter near the sink. "I'm going out to the barn to check on the ATVs for the tour this morning."

"I'm going with her," Max said.

As they left the lodge, Max held out his hand to JoJo.

She placed hers in it. JoJo liked the strength of his fingers wrapped around hers. "I did a headcount of the guests. We have more guests than ATVs. I'm not sure if all of them will want to ride."

"You and I can double up," Max suggested. "That will free up an ATV."

JoJo smiled. She liked that idea. Any time she could be close to Max was fine with her. "That works for me."

Once they were inside the barn, he pulled her into his arms. "I have to admit you're the best job I've ever had."

She laughed. "So, now I'm a job, huh?"

He grinned. "The best." And he kissed her.

JoJo was happier and more secure in his arms than she'd felt in a long time. And she didn't feel trapped. She knew that if she wanted out, all she had to do was say let go, and he'd immediately release her. Her sleep had been better the last two nights in his arms than she'd slept since the attack.

How would she sleep again when he went on to a real assignment? All of that kind of thinking would have to wait until after the ATV tour.

JoJo and Max doublechecked all of the vehicles, cranking them up and shutting them down. JoJo even checked for any oil leaks. The last thing she wanted was for one of the vehicles to die out on the trail.

When they were certain the four-wheelers were in good working order, they took care of the animals that needed morning care.

The campaign staff had the option to do one or all of the teambuilding activities. Each member had stated a preference to do all of the slated events to include the rope bridge, zipline and the ATV tour. The rope bridge would be first, followed by the zipline and, finally, the four-wheelers. Riding the trails was the last event before the group left for their dinner reservation in Fool's Gold that evening.

"You know, it's going to seem kind of quiet around here, after this group leaves," Max said.

JoJo nodded. "We're getting close to the end of the season. There will be a bit of a transition between summer and winter activities where there's a lull between them. It gives us time to get everything cleaned up, stored and pulled from storage for when it snows." Her lips twisted. "Then, I'll be working on snowmobiles instead of four-wheelers. Have to keep them running through the winter months for the tours RJ and I will lead through the forest and hills. Those tours don't usually start until late December or early January when there's plenty of snow on the trails."

When all the animals were taken care of and JoJo was satisfied the vehicles were in satisfactory condition, they joined the other ranch hands working the rope bridge and the zipline.

While some of the guests waited their turn on the ground, Gunny showed them how to rope a wooden steer.

Max and JoJo manned the rope bridge on either end.

Stover was the first to cross, followed by his

aide, Curry. Both men had been in the Army and were familiar with rope bridges. They made it across with no problem. Others were a little less steady.

One woman got halfway across and froze. JoJo walked out on the bridge and helped her to the other side.

When everyone had their chance to cross the bridge, they moved on to the zipline. Several of the campaign staff members opted out.

"No way." One woman shook her head and planted her feet firmly on the ground. "I'll stay here and wait for you guys to be done."

Again, Stover was first, followed by his aide. Then, one by one, the others slid down the zipline.

Emily stayed with the woman who'd opted out of the event.

The team adjourned for snacks in the lodge, while Max, RJ, JoJo and Jake pulled the ATVs out of the barn and lined them up.

The woman who'd refused to go on the zipline hurried up to Max where he stood beside JoJo. "I've never ridden a four-wheeler before. Will you be the one to show me how?" She batted her eyelashes.

JoJo fought to keep from rolling her eyes. Yes, Max knew how to drive a four-wheeler, but JoJo and RJ were the ones leading the tour. The woman was slender, with long blond hair and pretty blue eyes. Everything JoJo wasn't.

The woman turned to the closest vehicle. "Do you give individual lessons on how to drive these things?"

Max glanced toward JoJo.

JoJo shrugged. "I'm sure Max would be glad to help you."

Max gave her the briefest of frowns before turning a smile to the young woman. "I'm Max, by the way."

The blonde held out her hand. "Brianna." And they shook.

JoJo had the urge to slap the woman's hand away when she held onto Max's for a bit too long. Was this what jealousy felt like? Wow. She'd never felt like that before.

"I'd be happy to show you how to work the machine," Max said. And he led her over to the nearby four-wheeler and had her straddle the seat.

JoJo watched as he explained where the brakes and the throttle were and how to use them.

Meanwhile, JoJo, RJ, Jake, Cage and Gunny helped the others. After they'd given a brief round of instructions, they had each of the individuals drive around the barnyard to test their skills.

The four-wheelers were simple to operate, and everyone seemed to have it down by the time they left the barnyard and passed through the gate into the pasture. RJ led the group, and JoJo brought up the rear, with Max sitting behind her, his arms around her waist. She liked how thickly muscled his arms were and how secure she felt in them.

Brianna might have gotten instructions from Max, but JoJo had Max on the back of her ATV. She enjoyed a great amount of excitement and satisfaction in that fact. RJ led them up the path JoJo had explored a few days before, moving slowly in order to keep the guests together. They'd agreed to take them up to the bluff where the view of the Colorado Rockies was the most stunning of any other place on the ranch.

Stover followed RJ, Curry followed Stover, and the rest of his team fell in behind them. Since they had to go single file, they created a long chain of ATVs headed up into the mountains. Each guest had been told to keep the person in front of them in sight at all times. That way, no one would get lost on the trail.

At several points along the way, they had to slow even more than they were going already to allow people to catch up on the rocky patches that were a little more challenging than others. Everyone enjoyed splashing through a small stream and the short stop they made at the old mining ghost town.

When they finally reached the bluff, RJ had them park their ATVs far from the edge, up against a stand of evergreen trees. Guests walked to the bluff and stared out over the view as RJ explained to them which peaks they were looking at. Then she gave them a little history about the mining in the area and some of the original settlers.

When everyone seemed to have their fill of the view, they remounted their ATVs and RJ led the pack back.

Brianna couldn't get her ATV started, so Max went over to help her.

JoJo followed on foot.

Brianna stood beside the vehicle, wringing her hands as Max straddled the seat, checked the gear shift, clamped the brake, turned the key and hit the start button. It cranked for a second, and then died. When he tried the second time, it roared to life. He put it in neutral, set the brake and got off. "It's all yours."

Brianna backed away, holding up both hands. "I don't know if I can drive back. I'm looking at that downhill slope, and it's scaring me. Going up I was just fine," she said. "I don't know why but looking down that slope is making me dizzy."

"There's only one way off this mountain," JoJo said, "and that's to go back down."

Brianna shook her head. "Then I'll walk. I don't think that I could drive that ATV down the hill."

"Do you think you could ride on the back of one?" JoJo asked.

Brianna bit her lip. "I don't know. It's making me dizzy just looking down the path."

JoJo couldn't fault her. She'd run into people

who'd had that same issue. Going up, they were fine. Coming back down, they freaked out. Each time she'd been able to get them down from the mountain by having them ride on the back of somebody else's ATV with their eyes closed.

"You can ride with me," JoJo said. "All you have to do is hold on and keep your eyes closed. I'll get you down the mountain."

Brianna stared at JoJo. "But you're shorter than I am. I would still see the trail ahead of me."

"Not if you have your eyes closed," JoJo reminded her.

Brianna shook her head.

"Would you rather ride on the back with me?" Max offered.

JoJo's jaw tightened. The last thing she wanted was the pretty little female riding on the back of an ATV with Max, but then, they had to get moving or they'd lose sight of the rest of the group.

Brianna chewed on her lip a bit more, looking up at Max. "I think I might be able to ride down with Max," she said. "He would completely block my view of the trail below."

JoJo nodded. Max's broad shoulders would easily block her view. She cocked an eyebrow. "Are you up for that, Max?"

He nodded. "I'm up for it." He leaned close to JoJo and whispered, "But I'd rather ride with you." Then he gathered her into his arms and kissed her full on the lips in front of Brianna and the others who had yet to follow RJ from the top of the bluff. "Are you going to be all right?"

JoJo nodded. "I'll be fine."

"I'll be one ahead of you then," he said.

He mounted the vehicle.

Brianna mounted behind him and wrapped her arms around him, snuggling close.

JoJo ground her teeth as she climbed on board her ATV and cranked the engine. As they fell in line with the rest of them, JoJo hung back just a little bit with a view of the entire parade of vehicles. She counted. They'd started out with eighteen vehicles, counting hers. She moved along slowly, tallying the riders ahead of her. When she got to sixteen, she frowned. The seventeenth was her, and that was all there were. Somebody had been left behind.

The group kept moving down the hill and were just rounding a corner in the trail. JoJo thought about hurrying forward to catch up with Max to let him know that she'd be heading back to look for the straggler. But then she thought it would be faster if she just did it and then caught up.

She found a wide space in the trail, turned around and headed back up to the bluff. When she reached it, she couldn't find the other vehicle. She parked hers, got off and walked toward the tree line. The sun shone brightly on her, making the shadows even deeper beneath the trees. It wasn't until she'd reached the tree line that she saw the other vehicle. JoJo frowned. She didn't see the rider anywhere near the ATV.

As she approached the vehicle she called out. "Hello?" Thinking someone had had to make a pit stop in the woods, she didn't want to embarrass him or her. She called out again. "Hey, just answer me. Let me know who and where you are."

A twig snapped behind her. Before she could turn, arms clamped around her, trapping her arms within them. Someone taller and stronger than her lifted her off her feet and carried her toward the edge of the cliff. She fought, kicking and screaming as loud as she could, but she knew the people on the ATVs wouldn't hear them over the roar of their engines. Unless Max turned around and came back looking for her, she was on her own.

She only had seconds to spare before he reached the edge of the cliff. Focusing on the lessons she'd learned in Krav Maga with her feet dangling off the ground, all she could do was kick them, and her arms were completely trapped beneath his. With only one option left to her, she slammed her head back into his jaw as hard as she could.

Though pain shot through the back of her head, she ignored it.

Her captor swore, and his arms loosened.

JoJo pushed free of them and dropped to the ground. By then they were so near to the edge of the cliff, she was only steps away from falling over. She faced the man, and her eyes narrowed. "Curry, what are you doing?" she demanded, hoping to buy some time to figure out how to get around the bigger man.

He blocked her escape.

She had to do something to keep him from throwing her off the cliff.

"Tying up a loose end," he said.

She stared at him. This man did not have the light eyes of the one in her dreams, but her dream could've been wrong. "So, it was you?" she questioned. "You were the one who raped, beat, and buried me alive?"

He sneered. "One out of three."

"What do you mean? One out of three?"

He frowned. "I didn't rape or beat you. I was just cleaning up the mess."

"Then who?" At that moment, it came to her. "Stover?"

Curry snorted. "The man couldn't keep his dick in his pants. I was always the one who had to clean up after him."

"You mean there were others?" Her stomach roiled. "But you were the one who buried me in the sand?"

"Yeah, nobody would've found you if you'd have just died."

"But I didn't." Her lips pressed into a thin line. "Kind of put a kink in your plans, did I?"

"You had us worried for a while there." He took a step toward her.

She backed up one more and glanced over the edge of the cliff. She was only a foot away from falling off.

"We got a little worried there when we discovered you'd been found alive and evacuated to Ramstein, Germany. It wasn't until we learned that you had amnesia that we felt we had a little more time to take care of the loose ends. When Stover retired, he got this idiotic idea to run for political position. Lo and behold, he was running in his home state...where you landed. Couldn't have you remembering and ruining his chances and mine. So, like I said, just tying up loose ends." He lunged for her, his hands out, ready to push her over the edge.

JoJo grabbed his arm, bent and used his momentum to fling him over her shoulder. Her plan was to throw herself away from the edge of the cliff at the same time, but he latched onto her arm, and they both went over.

Curry released her as soon as he went over, but he'd already done the damage.

Closer to the rocky side of the bluff than Curry was, JoJo reached out, scrambling for purchase, praying that when she grabbed onto a rocky outcropping she had the strength to keep herself from falling all the way down the three-hundred-foot escarpment. Her knee hit a rocky protrusion, and as soon as her knee hit, her hands found it as she fell down. She clung, but her weight and her momentum jerked her hands free, and she continued her fall downward.

She was close to the side of the cliff, but it was sheer and straight down. JoJo found her life passing before her eyes. She would've laughed if she could have. But she really couldn't die. Not now. Not with Stover still loose.

Then she jolted to a stop. Not at the bottom, but on a very narrow ledge. Her feet found it, her knees buckled, and she almost fell over. For a moment she teetered on the brink. Just when she thought she'd tip backward and fall to her death, JoJo tipped forward against the rocky cliff.

She clung to it, shaking, her body bruised, her fingers bleeding, thanking God that she hadn't fallen to the bottom. She wasn't dead. She was alive. Now, all she had to do was wait for somebody to find her.

CHAPTER 16

THE PROBLEM with having Brianna ride on the back of his ATV was that Max couldn't turn far enough around to see how JoJo was coming along. It wasn't until they came to a bend in the trail that he was able to look back.

His heart fell to the pit of his belly. JoJo wasn't behind him. She was nowhere in sight. The trail was very narrow at the point. He couldn't turn around until he'd gone around the bend and found a wider place in the trail. When he started to turn, Brianna clutched at his waist.

"What are you doing?" she demanded.

"JoJo," he bit out, "she's not back there."

"She'll catch up," Briana insisted. "You need to keep following the people in front of us, or we'll get lost."

He shook his head. "We have to go back and get JoJo."

"But I don't want to go back up the hill. She'll be fine. She'll catch up with us."

"I'm going back," Max said.

"No," Briana fired back.

Max stopped the vehicle. "Get off!"

"What? You're not going to leave me here, are you?"

"Get off," he said. "Now!"

She slid off the back and stood in the middle of the trail. "You can't leave me like this."

Max didn't respond. He didn't care. He had to get back to JoJo. In his gut, he knew something was terribly wrong. He gave the ATV full throttle and blasted up the hillside to the top of the bluff. When he got there, he saw JoJo's ATV parked in the middle of the rise.

JoJo was nowhere to be seen.

He leaped off of his vehicle and yelled, "JoJo!" Max stopped to listen. When he didn't get a response, he ran to the edge of the cliff and looked down. His stomach clenched when he saw a body laying at the bottom. "JoJo!" he yelled. The body didn't move. As he studied it he knew it wasn't her. "JoJo!"

A small voice from below answered. "Max, I'm down here."

He leaned as far over the edge as he could without falling off. He spotted her clinging to the edge of a very narrow ledge, her body plastered against the stone escarpment. All it would take would be a brisk wind, and it could knock her off. She'd meet the same fate as whoever else it was at the bottom.

"Hang on, sweetheart. I'll come down to get you." He had nothing with him. No ropes. No rescue equipment. Nothing. And everybody else was on their way down the hill. He had to go catch up with them and get them to go for help. He had equipment in the back of his truck. If he could get to that, he could at least get down and stabilize her until a rescue team could get there to bring her up in a basket. "I have to go down the hill!" he shouted to her. "I'm going for help. Don't go anywhere."

A strangled laugh sounded from below. "I'll be here."

Max ran back to his ATV, hopped on and sped back down the hill. He had almost reached the corner where he'd looked back when RJ raced around it and nearly ran into him.

She came to a halt. "What's going on? Where's JoJo?"

"JoJo fell over the cliff."

"Holy shit!" RJ exclaimed.

"I need all of my equipment from the back of my truck. Ropes, D-rings and harnesses. Everything from behind the back seat of my truck. And I need you to call 9-1-1 and get a rescue team out here with a basket. Tell them we have one alive to be rescued and one to be recovered."

RJ's eyebrows rose. "Curry? He wasn't with the rest of the group."

Now that he thought about it, the person at the bottom of the cliff had worn the clothing colors Curry had been in. Max nodded.

RJ shook her head. "What the hell?"

"I'm sure we'll learn all about it once we get JoJo up from the cliff ledge. Right now, I need that equipment. ASAP."

They found a wide place in the trail and both turned. RJ headed downhill while Max headed back up to the cliff. He couldn't do much until he got his equipment, but he could stay there and provide encouragement until it arrived. Back at the top of the bluff, he parked his ATV, ran to the edge and lay down on his stomach so that he could scoot out as far as he could without falling over and keep an eye on her until help arrived. "I'm back," he called out. He could swear he heard a sob. "You hanging in there?"

"Doing the best I can," she answered. "Max?"

"Still with you, baby. Want to tell me what happened?"

"Curry," she said. "He tried to push me over." She laughed, her voice catching on a sob. "He succeeded."

"Why did he do it?"

"Dispose of the evidence," she said.

Max swore. "That bastard!"

"No kidding," she said. "He buried me, but he wasn't the one who beat and raped me."

The roar of an ATV drew Max's attention. He rolled onto his side to see who was headed their way. Hoping it was RJ, he was disappointed when he saw Stover pull up behind him. Then it hit him. If Curry was the one who'd buried her, and he wasn't the one who'd attacked her…

Max leapt to his feet and staggered a few steps on his bum leg. Stover didn't get off his ATV. Instead, he revved the engine and raced toward Max. He turned right before he got to Max and swung out his leg in an attempt to kick Max over the edge.

Max grabbed the man's leg and yanked Stover off his ATV.

Stover landed hard on his belly. Max threw himself on top of the man, straddled him and held him down. "It was you, wasn't it? You're sick and don't deserve to breathe the same air as JoJo."

Stover grunted. "I don't know what you're talking about. Get off of me."

"Your friend Curry pushed JoJo off the cliff. He told all."

"Why would he do that?" Stover said.

Max grabbed Stover's hair and pulled his head up. "Why would you try to kick me over the edge?"

"I thought it was you who'd pushed JoJo over the edge," Stover said. "You're the one who's a danger to others."

"Lying bastard." Max barely resisted the urge to slam Stover's face into the dirt.

"Is she dead?" Stover asked.

"Why do you want to know? Are you afraid she'll get her memories back and point to you as the man who raped and beat her?"

"Again, I don't know what you're talking about." Stover struggled beneath Max. "Get off me. I'll have you up on assault and battery charges."

"Your man Curry confessed before he threw JoJo over the edge."

"He did?" Stover asked. "Confessed what?"

"You know what," Max said. "I bet he'd be willing to confess in exchange for leniency on his sentence."

"You've got nothing on me," Stover said.

"Don't I?" Max called out, "You doing okay down there, JoJo?"

"Just waiting for my knight in shining armor to save me."

Stover muttered a curse.

Max leaned close to Stover's ear. "That's right, she's still alive, and she remembers."

Stover snorted. "It would be my word against hers."

"Her word and a rape kit." Max straddled Stover for fifteen more minutes until he heard the sound of engines climbing the hill. He kept up a running conversation with JoJo throughout that fifteen minutes, mostly to reassure himself that she was still alive and hadn't fallen the rest of the two-hundred-feet to her death.

She was getting weak, her voice shaking more with each passing minute.

Max could do nothing until he had his equipment.

Moments later, ATVs topped the hill, racing toward him. Gunny, RJ, Cage and Jake pulled to a skidding stop. In the basket of Gunny's ATV was all of Max's mountaineering gear. He couldn't get up until somebody relieved him of holding down Stover.

Jake ran over to where Max was. "I'll take over from here."

When Max got up, Stover tried to lunge to his feet. Jake pounced on him, put his knee in his back and slammed him into the dirt.

Max ran to Gunny's ATV and retrieved his mountaineering equipment. He checked each item carefully before tying off the rope on a tree, stepping into his harness and attaching his D-ring to the rope. Once he had his equipment in place, he stood on the edge of the cliff his heart racing, remembering the last time he'd rappelled.

"Hey, Max," JoJo called out.

"Yeah, JoJo."

"You've got this," she said. "Come on down and visit with me."

"I'm on my way." He stepped out over the ledge, let out a little rope, and then jumped. After several bounds, he ended up close to where she clung to the rock face of the bluff. Then he eased himself down to where they were even and walked sideways until he was right beside her. He stepped around her so that he was behind her, holding her up against the wall. "Hey, sweetheart," he said. "We've got to stop meeting this way."

She laughed and sobbed at the same time. "You did it."

He frowned. "Did what?"

"Faced your fear and conquered it." Her voice shook. "Congratulations."

"I didn't come down here to face my fear. I came after the woman who has captured my heart." He leaned close to her and pressed a kiss to her temple. "Okay, so yeah, I've faced my fear of ever falling in love, but I'm still afraid."

"Of what?" JoJo tried to turn her head, teetered and pressed her cheek against the stone wall.

Max leaned into her, holding her against the cliff. "I'm afraid she won't feel the same."

"Are you talking about me?" JoJo asked.

"You're the only one I've scaled a cliff to catch."

She shook her head slowly. "How could I have captured your heart? We've only known each other a few days."

"One of my buddies once told me that you'll know when you know. You don't need a month, a year, two years, you just know."

"How could you say that to me?"

"What? That I think I'm falling in love with you?"

"Yes." Tears welled in her eyes.

"Does it bother you?" he asked.

"Yes, it does." The tears slipped down her cheek.

"Why?"

"Because I can't turn around and throw my arms around you." She remained glued to the side of the cliff. "I'm even afraid to turn my face enough to look into your eyes. The ledge I'm standing on is barely wide enough for my feet."

"I've got your back, baby." He tied off his rope to anchor himself then he wrapped his arms around her. "I'm staying here with you," he said, "until the rescue team can get here."

"I heard Stover up there," she said. "What happened?"

Max's jaw hardened. "That bastard's going down."

"Good."

"Did they do a rape kit when you were in the hospital in Ramstein?" he asked.

"I assume they did," JoJo said. "I was just out of it for the first couple of days."

Max laughed. "Well, don't tell Stover that. I told him that they had a rape kit, and they could pin him with it."

"I should have known it was him. During my hypnosis session with Emily, I saw my attacker's eyes. They were light-colored, and his hair was kind of medium. Fits Stover."

"I bet we can get Hank and Swede to dig into Stover's deployments and they'll find out he was there at the same time you were. Any way it goes, Stover tried to push me over the edge of the cliff. That's attempted murder, in my books," Max said.

"My God, Max." JoJo tried to turn her head. Her foot slipped, and she would have fallen if Max wasn't holding her tightly

Max's grip tightened around her. "Don't worry. This old soldier still has some new tricks. I ended up pulling Stover off his ATV, and he landed flat on his face."

"Where is he now?" JoJo asked.

"Jake took over. He's holding him until we can get him down the mountain and into the hands of the sheriff's department."

"Hey, JoJo!" Gunny called out. "You hanging in there?"

JoJo laughed. "Yes, I am, Gunny."

"You better. I need help in the bar, and you're the best bartender I have."

"What about RJ?" JoJo asked.

"Oh, she's good too, but the customers like the way you mix drinks."

"I'll be back at work," she called out, "in time for the evening crowd. By the way, who's handling the lunch crowd?"

"I left Emily in charge," Gunny said.

"She'll be a better bartender than even I was," JoJo said. "She's good at listening."

"Hang in there," Gunny said. "The mountain rescue team is on its way."

JoJo leaned her head back against Max's shoulder. "Now that the man who attacked me has been identified, I won't need a bodyguard anymore."

Max squeezed her tighter. "You're not getting rid of me that easy."

"Good," she said. "That's the last thing I want to do because, you see, I kind of like you."

"What, you don't love me yet? It's been a whole what? Three or four days since we met? That's practically a lifetime." Max rested his cheek against her hair

"Based on everything that's happened to us since then? You're right."

He leaned forward and pressed his lips to her temple. "Sweetheart, take all the time you need to fall in love with me. Just as long as you do, because I'm pretty sure I'm well on my way to falling in love with you."

CHAPTER 17

JoJo sat on the porch swing at the lodge on Lost Valley Ranch with Max sitting beside her, holding her hand. Her heart was full, and she hadn't felt this relaxed and happy since she'd returned from her stay in the hospital in Germany.

"So what was it like to be hauled up the side of a cliff in a basket?" RJ asked.

"I'm not exactly sure," JoJo said. "I closed my eyes for most of it. What I do know is that I never want to do that again."

RJ frowned. "And I never want to see my dearest friend clinging to a ledge with barely enough room for a foot, much less two to keep her there without falling."

"I, for one, am thankful for that narrow ledge. It was the only thing between me, and the same fate Miles Curry suffered."

RJ shivered. "I can't tell you how hard I prayed that the wind didn't decide to make a showing at that moment."

JoJo lifted her chin. "So, what's going to happen to Stover?"

"For one, he won't be running for Congress," RJ said.

Jake nodded. "For another, Hank Patterson's computer guru, Swede, got hold of the hospital in Ramstein. They did process a rape kit on you. The DNA was a match for Lawrence Stover."

RJ's lip curled. "That bastard's going to jail."

JoJo nodded. "He's still claiming he's innocent."

"The DNA doesn't lie. We should get final results within the next couple of days. Swede also determined that Stover and Curry were at the same forward operating base during the time of your attack."

JoJo's breath caught and held in her throat. The two men had been trusted members of the US military. How could they have done what they had?

"Did you ever get your memory back from the attack?" RJ asked.

JoJo shook her head. "No, but I got enough back that I remembered the man beating me had light-colored eyes and medium-colored hair."

"It shouldn't matter," Jake said. "The DNA match from the rape kit sample will provide enough evidence to send Stover to prison at Leavenworth for a long time. And Curry isn't a problem anymore."

Max slipped an arm around JoJo's shoulders. "You're safe, now."

Emily sat on the porch stairs. "If you want, we can continue our hypnosis sessions to get those memories back."

JoJo shook her head. "No, I'd rather not. It's bad enough I have the nightmares without the hypnosis and will for a long time. Why bring it up even more? I know in my mind that Stover and Curry were responsible for what happened to me. Curry admitted it to me before he pushed me off the cliff."

Max's jaw hardened. "And Stover refuses to admit it. But we'll get him in court."

A car drove up in the lodge driveway.

JoJo glanced toward RJ. "Are we expecting anyone?"

RJ grinned. "Actually, we are. I got a call from Hank last night. He said he was sending Kujo down from Montana on a special mission." RJ lifted her chin. "You remember Kujo. He's one of Hank's Brotherhood Protectors. He's the one who came down to help set up the Colorado office. He has a special surprise for JoJo."

Jake smiled. "Swede tracked you back all the way to your unit, and then forward to the flight medics who airlifted you out to the medical staging unit. The flight medics have been taking care of someone special for you."

JoJo frowned. "I don't know what you're talking about."

"Swede spoke to the medics," Jake continued. "They said that some Afghan women found you and that a dog had been hanging around, protecting you."

JoJo nodded. "The dog dug me out and pulled on my arm until I rolled over and could breathe fresh air. I remember that. That dog saved my life. If he hadn't come along, those women wouldn't have found me."

Jake nodded. "One of the medics on board that helicopter thought that dog belonged to you. She loaded him into the helicopter with you. They've kept him safe and healthy until you could come back for him. When she found out where you'd landed in Colorado, she worked with a rescue organization to have the dog shipped to the States."

JoJo leaned forward. "Seriously?"

Kujo stepped out of the SUV and opened the back door. A German Shepherd jumped out.

JoJo frowned. "I'm almost sure that isn't the dog that dug me out of the dirt. It was more of a mutt. A mixed breed."

Jake grinned. "No, that's Kujo's dog, Six. Kujo rounded to the back of the SUV, opened the hatch and snapped a lead on an animal's collar.

A moment later, a dog about half the size of Six leaped to the ground. He had short, kind of yellow fur with one perky ear and one floppy one.

JoJo pushed to her feet, her eyes filling with tears. It was the dog that had saved her life. "It's him. I know it's him."

"The medics took good care of him while he was in Afghanistan. He's had all of his shots, he's been dewormed and treated for parasites and fleas," Jake said. "All he needs is a good home with someone who will treat him well."

JoJo stepped down from the porch, her heart swelling in her chest. "But he's not my dog," she whispered.

Kujo walked with the dog to the deck and smiled up at everyone. "Were you waiting for me to start the party?"

Gunny laughed. "Sorry, Kujo, we started the party without you."

"No worries," Kujo said. "I brought a friend for JoJo. Seems they've met before." He grinned. "The medics who airlifted you to the medical staging unit have taken care of your dog since you left over six months ago."

"Actually, that dog doesn't belong to me," JoJo said, squatting in front of him to scratch behind his ears.

"He can be," Jake said.

She looked up at Jake, her eyes shining. "What's his name?"

"The medics named him Roscoe. But if you decide to take him, you can name him anything you want."

JoJo smiled. "Roscoe's a good name. I like it. But what am I going to do with a dog when I move back to my apartment?"

"You're not going back to that apartment, or any other apartment," RJ insisted.

"You're staying here at the Lost Valley Ranch. At least, for now," Max said.

RJ grinned. "Is there something you need to tell us?"

Max shook his head. "Not yet, but soon."

"Roscoe is welcome to stay here at Lost Valley Ranch," RJ said. "From what Swede said, the medics who kept him put him through some training. He's got some manners."

JoJo held out her hand for Roscoe to sniff.

After investigating her hand, he let out a slight yipping sound and jumped up on her.

JoJo fell backward on her bottom.

"Are you sure you want this dog?" Kujo asked, giving her a hand up.

"Yes," JoJo said. "I owe this dog my life." She bent and tentatively wrapped her arms around the dog and hugged it close.

Roscoe didn't seem to mind. He rested his chin on her shoulder and panted.

"Thank you for saving me," JoJo whispered into the dog's ear.

Max stepped up beside JoJo and the dog.

JoJo looked up at the former Special Operations soldier. "Looks like we have a dog." She was so happy, she didn't care who was watching. She flung her arms around Max's neck, leaned up on her toes and kissed Max.

"What was that for?" he asked. "Not that I'm complaining."

"You and Roscoe have something in common," she said.

Max cocked an eyebrow. "Oh yeah? And what would that be?"

"You both saved my life."

Max chuckled. "Whew, I thought for a moment you'd say we smell like each other." He winked.

JoJo shook her head. "It's a good thing I don't love you for your jokes. You'd never make a living as a comedian."

"You mean my stand-up comedy isn't even getting a chuckle out of you?"

"Nope," JoJo said.

Max's eyebrows drew downward into a V. "Wait. What was it you said?"

JoJo's opened her eyes wide, looking all innocent, her cheeks heating. "About you never making a living as a comedian?"

"No, the part about not loving me for my jokes." He pulled her into his arms. "Does that mean you love me for some other reason?"

"I wouldn't say that." She twisted her lips.

Max's frowned deepened. "So what does it mean?"

She wrapped her arms around his neck and smiled up into his eyes. "It means I love you for all the other reasons I could possibly name."

He laughed and hugged her tight. "I thought you didn't think we could fall in love in such a short timeframe."

"Like you said...when you know you know." She leaned up on her toes. "I hope you like me, and I hope you like dogs. I'm a package deal." She rested her hand on Roscoe's head. "Me and Roscoe."

Max kissed her and stared into her eyes. "I'll take the package deal. I love you, JoJo. I want to spend the rest of my life getting to know everything there is to know about you."

"And I want to spend the rest of my life getting to know you," she said. "I feel like my life has been on hold. Until I met you. I've faced my fears and conquered them because of you. Now, I want to embrace my life and move on."

Max rested his forehead against hers. "As long as you move on with me, I'll be happy."

THE END

Interested in more military romance stories?
Subscribe to my newsletter and receive the Military
Heroes Box Set
Subscribe Here

BREAKING SILENCE

DELTA FORCE STRONG BOOK #1

New York Times & *USA Today*
Bestselling Author

BREAKING
Silence
DELTA FORCE
STRONG
New York Times & USA Today Bestselling Author
ELLE JAMES

CHAPTER 1

HAD he known they would be deployed so soon after their last short mission to El Salvador, Rucker Sloan wouldn't have bought that dirt bike from his friend Duff. Now, it would sit there for months before he actually got to take it out to the track.

The team had been given forty-eight hours to pack their shit, take care of business and get onto the C130 that would transport them to Afghanistan.

Now, boots on the ground, duffel bags stowed in their assigned quarters behind the wire, they were ready to take on any mission the powers that be saw fit to assign.

What he wanted most that morning, after being awake for the past thirty-six hours, was a cup of strong, black coffee.

The rest of his team had hit the sack as soon as they got in. Rucker had already met with their commanding officer, gotten a brief introduction to the regional issues and had been told to get some rest. They'd be operational within the next forty-eight hours.

Too wound up to sleep, Rucker followed a stream of people he hoped were heading for the chow hall. He should be able to get coffee there.

On the way, he passed a sand volleyball court where two teams played against each other. One of the teams had four players, the other only three. The four-person squad slammed a ball to the ground on the other side of the net. The only female player ran after it as it rolled toward Rucker.

He stopped the ball with his foot and picked it up.

The woman was tall, slender, blond-haired and blue-eyed. She wore an Army PT uniform of shorts and an Army T-shirt with her hair secured back from her face in a ponytail seated on the crown of her head.

Without makeup, and sporting a sheen of perspiration, she was sexy as hell, and the men on both teams knew it.

They groaned when Rucker handed her the ball. He'd robbed them of watching the female soldier bending over to retrieve the runaway.

She took the ball and frowned. "Do you play?"

"I have," he answered.

"We could use a fourth." She lifted her chin in challenge.

Tired from being awake for the past thirty-six hours, Rucker opened his mouth to say *hell no*. But he made the mistake of looking into her sky-blue eyes and instead said, "I'm in."

What the hell was he thinking?

Well, hadn't he been wound up from too many hours sitting in transit? What he needed was a little physical activity to relax his mind and muscles. At least, that's what he told himself in the split-second it took to step into the sandbox and serve up a heaping helping of whoop-ass.

He served six times before the team playing opposite finally returned one. In between each serve, his side gave him high-fives, all members except one—the blonde with the blue eyes he stood behind, admiring the length of her legs beneath her black Army PT shorts.

Twenty minutes later, Rucker's team won the match. The teams broke up and scattered to get showers or breakfast in the chow hall.

"Can I buy you a cup of coffee?" the pretty blonde asked.

"Only if you tell me your name." He twisted his lips into a wry grin. "I'd like to know who delivered those wicked spikes."

She held out her hand. "Nora Michaels," she said.

He gripped her hand in his, pleased to feel firm pressure. Women might be the weaker sex, but he didn't like a dead fish handshake from males or females. Firm and confident was what he preferred. Like her ass in those shorts.

She cocked an eyebrow. "And you are?"

He'd been so intent thinking about her legs and ass, he'd forgotten to introduce himself. "Rucker Sloan. Just got in less than an hour ago."

"Then you could probably use a tour guide to the nearest coffee."

He nodded. "Running on fumes here. Good coffee will help."

"I don't know about good, but it's coffee and it's fresh." She released his hand and fell in step beside him, heading in the direction of some of the others from their volleyball game.

"As long as it's strong and black, I'll be happy."

She laughed. "And awake for the next twenty-four hours."

"Spoken from experience?" he asked, casting a glance in her direction.

She nodded. "I work nights in the medical facility. It can be really boring and hard to stay awake when we don't have any patients to look after." She held up her hands. "Not that I want any of our boys injured and in need of our care."

"But it does get boring," he guessed.

"It makes for a long deployment." She held out her hand. "Nice to meet you, Rucker. Is Rucker a call sign or your real name?"

He grinned. "Real name. That was the only thing

my father gave me before he cut out and left my mother and me to make it on our own."

"Your mother raised you, and you still joined the Army?" She raised an eyebrow. "Most mothers don't want their boys to go off to war."

"It was that or join a gang and end up dead in a gutter," he said. "She couldn't afford to send me to college. I was headed down the gang path when she gave me the ultimatum. Join and get the GI-Bill, or she would cut me off and I'd be out in the streets. To her, it was the only way to get me out of L.A. and to have the potential to go to college someday."

She smiled "And you stayed in the military."

He nodded. "I found a brotherhood that was better than any gang membership in LA. For now, I take college classes online. It was my mother's dream for me to graduate college. She never went, and she wanted so much more for me than the streets of L.A.. When my gig is up with the Army, if I haven't finished my degree, I'll go to college fulltime."

"And major in what?" Nora asked.

"Business management. I'm going to own my own security service. I want to put my combat skills to use helping people who need dedicated and specialized protection."

Nora nodded. "Sounds like a good plan."

"I know the protection side of things. I need to learn the business side and business law. Life will be different on the civilian side."

"True."

"How about you? What made you sign up?" he asked.

She shrugged. "I wanted to put my nursing degree to good use and help our men and women in uniform. This is my first assignment after training."

"Drinking from the firehose?" Rucker stopped in front of the door to the mess hall.

She nodded. "Yes. But it's the best baptism under fire medical personnel can get. I'll be a better nurse for it when I return to the States."

"How much longer do you have to go?" he asked, hoping that she'd say she'd be there as long as he was. In his case, he never knew how long their deployments would last. One week, one month, six months...

She gave him a lopsided smile. "I ship out in a week."

"That's too bad." He opened the door for her. "I just got here. That doesn't give us much time to get to know each other."

"That's just as well." Nora stepped through the door. "I don't want to be accused of fraternizing. I'm too close to going back to spoil my record."

Rucker chuckled. "Playing volleyball and sharing a table while drinking coffee won't get you written up. I like the way you play. I'm curious to know where you learned to spike like that."

"I guess that's reasonable. Coffee first." She led him into the chow hall.

The smells of food and coffee made Rucker's mouth water.

He grabbed a tray and loaded his plate with eggs, toast and pancakes drenched in syrup. Last, he stopped at the coffee urn and filled his cup with freshly brewed black coffee.

When he looked around, he found Nora seated at one of the tables, holding a mug in her hands, a small plate with cottage cheese and peaches on it.

He strode over to her. "Mind if I join you?"

"As long as you don't hit on me," she said with cocked eyebrows.

"You say that as if you've been hit on before."

She nodded and sipped her steaming brew. "I lost count how many times in the first week I was here."

"Shows they have good taste in women and, unfortunately, limited manners."

"And you're better?" she asked, a smile twitching the corners of her lips.

"I'm not hitting on you. You can tell me to leave, and I'll be out of this chair so fast, you won't have time to enunciate the V."

She stared straight into his eyes, canted her head to one side and said, "Leave."

In the middle of cutting into one of his pancakes, Rucker dropped his knife and fork on the tray, shot out of his chair and left with his tray, sloshing coffee as he moved. He hoped she was just testing him. If she wasn't…oh, well. He was used to eating meals alone. If she was, she'd have to come to him.

He took a seat at the next table, his back to her, and resumed cutting into his pancake.

Nora didn't utter a word behind him.

Oh, well. He popped a bite of syrupy sweet pancake in his mouth and chewed thoughtfully. She was only there for another week. Man, she had a nice ass…and those legs… He sighed and bent over his plate to stab his fork into a sausage link.

"This chair taken?" a soft, female voice sounded in front of him.

He looked up to see the pretty blond nurse standing there with her tray in her hands, a crooked smile on her face.

He lifted his chin in silent acknowledgement.

She laid her tray on the table and settled onto the chair. "I didn't think you'd do it."

"Fair enough. You don't know me," he said.

"I know that you joined the Army to get out of street life. That your mother raised you after your father skipped out, that you're working toward a business degree and that your name is Rucker." She sipped her coffee.

He nodded, secretly pleased she'd remembered all that. Maybe there was hope for getting to know the pretty nurse before she redeployed to the States. And who knew? They might run into each other on the other side of the pond.

Still, he couldn't show too much interest, or he'd be no better than the other guys who'd hit on her. "Since you're redeploying back to the States in a week, and I'm due to go out on a mission, probably within the next twenty-four to forty-eight hours, I don't know if it's worth our time to get to know each other any more than we already have."

She nodded. "I guess that's why I want to sit with you. You're not a danger to my perfect record of no fraternizing. I don't have to worry that you'll fall in love with me in such a short amount of time." She winked.

He chuckled. "As I'm sure half of this base has fallen in love with you since you've been here."

She shrugged. "I don't know if it's love, but it's damned annoying."

"How so?"

She rolled her eyes toward the ceiling. "I get flowers left on my door every day."

"And that's annoying? I'm sure it's not easy coming up with flowers out here in the desert." He set down his fork and took up his coffee mug. "I think it's sweet." He held back a smile. Well, almost.

"They're hand-drawn on notepad paper and left on the door of my quarters and on the door to the shower tent." She shook her head. "It's kind of creepy and stalkerish."

Rucker nodded. "I see your point. The guys should at least have tried their hands at origami flowers, since the real things are scarce around here."

Nora smiled. "I'm not worried about the pictures, but the line for sick call is ridiculous."

"How so?"

"So many of the guys come up with the lamest excuses to come in and hit on me. I asked to work the nightshift to avoid sick call altogether."

"You have a fan group." He smiled. "Has the adoration gone to your head?"

She snorted softly. "No."

"You didn't get this kind of reaction back in the States?"

"I haven't been on active duty for long. I only decided to join the Army after my mother passed away. I was her fulltime nurse for a couple years as she went through stage four breast cancer. We thought she might make it." Her shoulders sagged. "But she didn't."

"I'm sorry to hear that. My mother meant a lot to me, as well. I sent money home every month after I enlisted and kept sending it up until the day she died suddenly of an aneurysm."

"I'm so sorry about your mother's passing," Nora said, shaking her head. "Wow. As an enlisted man, how did you make enough to send some home?"

"I ate in the chow hall and lived on post. I didn't

party or spend money on civilian clothes or booze. Mom needed it. I gave it to her."

"You were a good son to her," Nora said.

His chest tightened. "She died of an aneurysm a couple of weeks before she was due to move to Texas where I'd purchased a house for her."

"Wow. And, let me guess, you blame yourself for not getting her to Texas sooner...?" Her gaze captured his.

Her words hit home, and he winced. "Yeah. I should've done it sooner."

"Can't bring people back with regrets." Nora stared into her coffee cup. "I learned that. The only thing I could do was move forward and get on with living. I wanted to get away from Milwaukee and the home I'd shared with my mother. Not knowing where else to go, I wandered past a realtor's office and stepped into a recruiter's office. I had my nursing degree, they wanted and needed nurses on active duty. I signed up, they put me through some officer training and here I am." She held her arms out.

"Playing volleyball in Afghanistan, working on your tan during the day and helping soldiers at night." Rucker gave her a brief smile. "I, for one, appreciate what you're doing for our guys and gals."

"I do the best I can," she said softly. "I just wish I could do more. I'd rather stay here than redeploy back to the States, but they're afraid if they keep us here too long, we'll burn out or get PTSD."

"One week, huh?"

She nodded. "One week."

"In my field, one week to redeploy back to the States is a dangerous time. Anything can happen and usually does."

"Yeah, but you guys are on the frontlines, if not behind enemy lines. I'm back here. What could happen?"

Rucker flinched. "Oh, sweetheart, you didn't just say that…" He glanced around, hoping no one heard her tempt fate with those dreaded words *What could happen?*

Nora grinned. "You're not superstitious, are you?"

"In what we do, we can't afford not to be," he said, tossing salt over his shoulder.

"I'll be fine," she said in a reassuring, nurse's voice.

"Stop," he said, holding up his hand. "You're only digging the hole deeper." He tossed more salt over his other shoulder.

Nora laughed.

"Don't laugh." He handed her the saltshaker. "Do it."

"I'm not tossing salt over my shoulder. Someone has to clean the mess hall."

Rucker leaned close and shook salt over her shoulder. "I don't know if it counts if someone else throws salt over your shoulder, but I figure you now need every bit of luck you can get."

"You're a fighter but afraid of a little bad luck."

Nora shook her head. "Those two things don't seem to go together."

"You'd be surprised how easily my guys are freaked by the littlest things."

"And you," she reminded him.

"You asking *what could happen?* isn't a little thing. That's in-your-face tempting fate." Rucker was laying it on thick to keep her grinning, but deep down, he believed what he was saying. And it didn't make a difference the amount of education he had or the statistics that predicted outcomes. His gut told him she'd just tempted fate with her statement. Maybe he was overthinking things. Now, he was worried she wouldn't make it back to the States alive.

NORA LIKED RUCKER. He was the first guy who'd walked away without an argument since she'd arrived at the base in Afghanistan. He'd meant what he'd said and proved it. His dark brown hair and deep green eyes, coupled with broad shoulders and a narrow waist, made him even more attractive. Not all the men were in as good a shape as Rucker. And he seemed to have a very determined attitude.

She hadn't known what to expect when she'd deployed. Being the center of attention of almost every single male on the base hadn't been one of her expectations. She'd only ever considered herself average in the looks department. But when the men outnumbered women by more than ten to one, she guessed average appearance moved up in the ranks.

"Where did you learn to play volleyball?" Rucker asked, changing the subject of her leaving and her flippant comment about what could happen in one week.

"I was on the volleyball team in high school. It got me a scholarship to a small university in my home state of Minnesota, where I got my Bachelor of Science degree in Nursing."

"It takes someone special to be a nurse," he stated. "Is that what you always wanted to be?"

She shook her head. "I wanted to be a firefighter when I was in high school."

"What made you change your mind?"

She stared down at the coffee growing cold in her mug. "My mother was diagnosed with cancer when I was a senior in high school. I wanted to help but felt like I didn't know enough to be of assistance." She looked up. "She made it through chemo and radiation treatments and still came to all of my volleyball games. I thought she was in the clear."

"She wasn't?" Rucker asked, his tone low and gentle.

"She didn't tell me any different. When I got the scholarship, I told her I wanted to stay close to home to be with her. She insisted I go and play volleyball for the university. I was pretty good and played for the first two years I was there. I quit the team in my third year to start the nursing program. I didn't know there was anything wrong back home. I called every week to talk to Mom. She never let on that she was sick." She forced a smile. "But you don't want my sob story. You probably want to know what's going on around here."

He set his mug on the table. "If we were alone in a coffee bar back in the States, I'd reach across the table and take your hand."

"Oh, please. Don't do that." She looked around the mess hall, half expecting someone might have overheard Rucker's comment. "You're enlisted. I'm an officer. That would get us into a whole lot of trouble."

"Yeah, but we're also two human beings. I wouldn't be human if I didn't feel empathy for you and want to provide comfort."

She set her coffee cup on the table and laid her hands in her lap. "I'll be satisfied with the thought. Thank you."

"Doesn't seem like enough. When did you find out your mother was sick?"

She swallowed the sadness that welled in her throat every time she remembered coming home to find out her mother had been keeping her illness from her. "It wasn't until I went home for Christmas in my senior year that I realized she'd been lying to me for a while." She laughed in lieu of sobbing. "I don't care who they are, old people don't always tell the truth."

"How long had she been keeping her sickness from you?"

"She'd known the cancer had returned halfway through my junior year. I hadn't gone home that summer because I'd been working hard to get my coursework and clinical hours in the nursing program. When I went home at Christmas…" Nora gulped. "She wasn't the same person. She'd lost so much weight and looked twenty years older."

"Did you stay home that last semester?" Rucker asked.

"Mom insisted I go back to school and finish what I'd started. Like your mother, she hadn't gone to college. She wanted her only child to graduate. She was afraid that if I stayed home to take care of her, I wouldn't finish my nursing degree."

"I heard from a buddy of mine that those programs can be hard to get into," he said. "I can see why she wouldn't want you to drop everything in your life to take care of her."

Nora gave him a watery smile. "That's what she said. As soon as my last final was over, I returned to my hometown. I became her nurse. She lasted another three months before she slipped away."

"That's when you joined the Army?"

She shook her head. "Dad was so heartbroken, I stayed a few months until he was feeling better. I got a job at a local emergency room. On weekends, my father and I worked on cleaning out the house and getting it ready to put on the market."

"Is your dad still alive?" Rucker asked.

Nora nodded. "He lives in Texas. He moved to a small house with a big backyard." She forced a smile. "He has a garden, and all the ladies in his retirement community think he's the cat's meow. He still misses Mom, but he's getting on with his life."

Rucker tilted his head. "When did you join the military?"

"When Dad sold the house and moved into his retirement community. I worried about him, but he's doing better."

"And you?"

"I miss her. But she'd whip my ass if I wallowed in self-pity for more than a moment. She was a strong woman and expected me to be the same."

Rucker grinned. "From what I've seen, you are."

Nora gave him a skeptical look. "You've only seen me playing volleyball. It's just a game." Not that she'd admit it, but she was a real softy when it came to caring for the sick and injured.

"If you're half as good at nursing, which I'm willing to bet you are, you're amazing." He started to reach across the table for her hand. Before he actually touched her, he grabbed the saltshaker and shook it over his cold breakfast.

"You just got in this morning?" Nora asked.

Rucker nodded.

"How long will you be here?" she asked.

"I don't know."

"What do you mean, you don't know? I thought when people were deployed, they were given a specific timeframe."

"Most people are. We're deployed where and when needed."

Nora frowned. "What are you? Some kind of special forces team?"

His lips pressed together. "Can't say."

She sat back. He was some kind of Special Forces. "Army, right?"

He nodded.

That would make him Delta Force. The elite of the elite. A very skilled soldier who undertook incredibly dangerous missions. She gulped and stopped herself from reaching across the table to take his hand. "Well, I hope all goes well while you and your team are here."

"Thanks."

A man hurried across the chow hall wearing shorts and an Army T-shirt. He headed directly toward their table.

Nora didn't recognize him. "Expecting someone?" she asked Rucker, tipping her head toward the man.

Rucker turned, a frown pulling his eyebrows together. "Why the hell's Dash awake?"

Nora frowned. "Dash? Please tell me that's his callsign, not his real name."

Rucker laughed. "It should be his real name. He's first into the fight, and he's fast." Rucker stood and faced his teammate. "What's up?"

"CO wants us all in the Tactical Operations Center," Dash said. "On the double."

"Guess that's my cue to exit." Rucker turned to Nora. "I enjoyed our talk."

She nodded. "Me, too."

Dash grinned. "Tell you what...I'll stay and finish your conversation while you see what the commander wants."

Rucker hooked Dash's arm twisted it up behind his back, and gave him a shove toward the door. "You heard the CO, he wants all of us." Rucker winked at Nora. "I hope to see you on the volleyball court before you leave."

"Same. Good luck." Nora's gaze followed Rucker's broad shoulders and tight ass out of the chow hall. Too bad she'd only be there another week before she shipped out. She would've enjoyed more volleyball and coffee with the Delta Force operative.

He'd probably be on maneuvers that entire week.

She stacked her tray and coffee cup in the collection area and left the chow hall, heading for the building where she shared her quarters with Beth Drennan, a nurse she'd become friends with during their deployment together.

As close as they were, Nora didn't bring up her conversation with the Delta. With only a week left at the base, she probably wouldn't run into him again. Though she would like to see him again, she prayed he didn't end up in the hospital.

Breaking Silence

ABOUT THE AUTHOR

ELLE JAMES also writing as MYLA JACKSON is a *New York Times* and *USA Today* Bestselling author of books including cowboys, intrigues and paranormal adventures that keep her readers on the edges of their seats. When she's not at her computer, she's traveling, snow skiing, boating, or riding her ATV, dreaming up new stories. Learn more about Elle James at www.ellejames.com

Website | Facebook | Twitter | GoodReads | Newsletter | BookBub | Amazon

Or visit her alter ego Myla Jackson at mylajackson.com
Website | Facebook | Twitter | Newsletter

Follow Me!
www.ellejames.com
ellejames@ellejames.com

Warrior's Resolve (#5)

Brotherhood Protectors Series

Montana SEAL (#1)

Bride Protector SEAL (#2)

Montana D-Force (#3)

Cowboy D-Force (#4)

Montana Ranger (#5)

Montana Dog Soldier (#6)

Montana SEAL Daddy (#7)

Montana Ranger's Wedding Vow (#8)

Montana SEAL Undercover Daddy (#9)

Cape Cod SEAL Rescue (#10)

Montana SEAL Friendly Fire (#11)

Montana SEAL's Mail-Order Bride (#12)

SEAL Justice (#13)

Ranger Creed (#14)

Delta Force Rescue (#15)

Dog Days of Christmas (#16)

Montana Rescue (Sleeper SEAL)

Hot SEAL Salty Dog (SEALs in Paradise)

Hot SEAL,Hawaiian Nights (SEALs in Paradise)

Hot SEAL Bachelor Party (SEALs in Paradise)

Hot SEAL, Independence Day (SEALs in Paradise)

Brotherhood Protectors Vol 1

The Billionaire Husband Test (#1)

The Billionaire Cinderella Test (#2)

The Billionaire Bride Test (#3)

The Billionaire Daddy Test (#4)

The Billionaire Matchmaker Test (#5)

The Billionaire Glitch Date (#6)

The Billionaire Perfect Date (#7) coming soon

The Billionaire Replacement Date (#8) coming soon

The Billionaire Wedding Date (#9) coming soon

Ballistic Cowboy

Hot Combat (#1)

Hot Target (#2)

Hot Zone (#3)

Hot Velocity (#4)

Cajun Magic Mystery Series

Voodoo on the Bayou (#1)

Voodoo for Two (#2)

Deja Voodoo (#3)

Cajun Magic Mysteries Books 1-3

SEAL Of My Own

Navy SEAL Survival

Navy SEAL Captive

Navy SEAL To Die For

Navy SEAL Six Pack

Devil's Shroud Series

Deadly Reckoning (#1)

Deadly Engagement (#2)

Deadly Liaisons (#3)

Deadly Allure (#4)

Deadly Obsession (#5)

Deadly Fall (#6)

Covert Cowboys Inc Series

Triggered (#1)

Taking Aim (#2)

Bodyguard Under Fire (#3)

Cowboy Resurrected (#4)

Navy SEAL Justice (#5)

Navy SEAL Newlywed (#6)

High Country Hideout (#7)

Clandestine Christmas (#8)

Thunder Horse Series

Hostage to Thunder Horse (#1)

Thunder Horse Heritage (#2)

Thunder Horse Redemption (#3)

Christmas at Thunder Horse Ranch (#4)

Demon Series

Hot Demon Nights (#1)

Demon's Embrace (#2)

Tempting the Demon (#3)

Lords of the Underworld

Witch's Initiation (#1)

Witch's Seduction (#2)

The Witch's Desire (#3)

Possessing the Witch (#4)

Stealth Operations Specialists (SOS)

Nick of Time

Alaskan Fantasy

Boys Behaving Badly Anthology

Rogues (#1)

Blue Collar (#2)

Pirates (#3)

Stranded (#4)

First Responder (#5)

Blown Away

Warrior's Conquest

Enslaved by the Viking Short Story

Conquests

Smokin' Hot Firemen

Protecting the Colton Bride

Protecting the Colton Bride & Colton's Cowboy Code

Heir to Murder

Secret Service Rescue

High Octane Heroes

Haunted

Engaged with the Boss

Cowboy Brigade

Time Raiders: The Whisper

Bundle of Trouble

Killer Body

Operation XOXO

An Unexpected Clue

Baby Bling

Under Suspicion, With Child

Texas-Size Secrets

Cowboy Sanctuary

Lakota Baby

Dakota Meltdown

Beneath the Texas Moon